For Mom

*Thank you for
your guidance and
your love.*

Wild Hearts Elephant Sanctuary Book 2

I AM JANE

April O'Connell

ISBN: 978-1-945169-36-6

Orison Publishers, Inc.
PO Box 188
Grantham, PA 17027
717-731-1405
www.OrisonPublishers.com
Publish your book now, marsha@orisonpublishers.com

Printed in the United States of America

Acknowledgements

Thank you, Marsha Blessing with Orison Publishers, Inc., you truly are a blessing.

CHAPTER 1

January 1938

I like the way the clouds, with their rolling white plumes, softly cover the tops of the African mountains. As they give way to the sun that begins to peek out of its hiding place, another quickly passing storm has offered a light cooling breeze that is carrying the ominous clouds, causing them to disappear out of my sight, and with it, the heavy rains have changed to a soft mist that cools my skin.

The steamy droplets seemed to blanket the earth in a refreshing sheet of calmness. The rains washed everything anew. Dripping water thumped the roof of my porch to make a light drumming sound that is both soothing and pleasing. As I close my eyes and listen, the beating rhythm reminds me of the tribal drums I often hear in the distance, deep within the jungle. I hear their music from time to time and wonder about them. It begins as lightly as the mist but builds in intensity and volume, like the rolling thunder over the mountains.

I've heard the stories of the rival tribes that would kill you with their poison darts. Father told me once that the poison is so potent that a person would be dead before they hit the ground. When I hear the drumbeats, I can't be sure if the tribes are in celebration or at war. It could be both. I have never had a reason or been brave enough to cross into the tribes' proclaimed parts of the jungle. They prefer to stay hidden. With respect for them, I am content to listen to their drumming and remember the stories told to me about them by select scientists and travelers that have visited the tribes and lived to tell about it.

Steam was rising from the water that has hit the heated, dry, cracked ground, which drinks it's fill until murky puddles form. The cloudy water was too enticing to resist for my six-year-old daughter, Olivia.

She was restless beside me. Her little hands were clamped on her lap and she was continuously glancing from me to the muddy puddle. Olivia clears her throat as a signal that she has lost all patience. "Mommy?"

"Yes, Olivia."

"Why must I wait until the rain slows down? I get wet either way. It's quicker to dance in the rain when it pours. That way I never have to wait."

"Patience is something that you must learn."

"But why do I have to wait if I already know what I want to do?"

I smiled down at Olivia, remembering similar scenes with my own mother when I was her age. "You may go, Olivia," I said caving to her plea.

"Yah!" She shrieked and jumped off the porch, smiling as she twirled herself in circles, splashing her bare legs that soon become as muddy as the earth. She was giggling and squealing with delight. As Olivia lifted her head skyward and opened her mouth, she tried to catch the cooling, sparse liquid on her tongue.

Olivia's wild spirit matches my own. "Look, Mommy! Look at the pretty sky," she pointed heavenward. "It has lots of colors today."

"I see that. Why do you think the sky has all those pretty colors?"

"Because God is just as tired of the rain as I am." Olivia nodded her head.

As I watch her spin and dance, I try to recall my life at six-years-old. It's not as vivid as some other youthful years. Some memories will be forever etched into my mind. Important life lessons that center around the work we do at Wild Hearts Elephant Sanctuary and the time when I was kidnapped by poachers. That is something that haunts me every night.

During the day, I can control my thoughts and not let myself be dragged into the hell that awaits me at night. During the day, I am busy with the elephants, my home, the children, and my husband, Matt. It is the nightmarish dreams that invade my sleep and torture my mind when I am vulnerable.

I shook my head to rid my mind and not allow those thoughts to control my day.

I am just trying to relax and enjoy watching Olivia play and discover. Everything is an innocent game to her. She can be amused easily with her wild imagination. Whether she is exploring the barns that house the new arrival of elephants or is riding on the back of her favorite elephant, Kendi, she is full of constant movement. Like a bee pollinating the wildflowers that never stops long enough to smell their scent. Olivia buzzes with enthusiastic energy.

Olivia is jumping up and down in a puddle, bouncing the curls on her little golden-colored head. Her play clothes are wet and mud-covered from her non-stop activity. "Look at me, Mommy. I'm an elephant!" Olivia exclaimed while standing in a seven-inch-deep puddle that's up to her shins. She is near the porch, stomping her feet and causing mud to fly everywhere. It splattered my legs and I used my hand to wipe it from my leg and my son Charlie's arm.

Charlie, who has just turned two-years-old, is not content to watch his big sister from my lap. He was beginning to squirm and trying to lower himself. I readjusted him higher on my lap, hoping to keep him dry and clean for just a few minutes longer. My motives were also to avoid a sibling confrontation that would ensue when Charlie tries to play with Olivia. The constant battle of siblings exhausts my patience.

We watch as Olivia uses her little arm as a trunk, swinging it back and forth into the puddle and raising it over her head, dribbling mud into her hair. She repeats the process. Quickly, her arms are as covered as her chubby little legs. I do not care. I love that Olivia is fascinated with nature as much as I am. The dirt will wash away—the memories will stay with me forever.

Charlie is wriggling and fussing to get down and play with his older sister. I know that it is unfair not to permit him the same freedom that I give to Olivia, so I allowed him to slide down my legs and onto the bottom porch step. He smiled at the prospect of mud and big sister playtime.

"No!" Olivia stamped her foot and stood with her arms crossed in protest. "No, Charlie, you can't be an elephant with me. You're too small," Olivia objected.

"I can," Charlie answered with a nod of his head.

Charlie does whatever makes his little heart happy. He looked up at his sister with a big smile and copied her movements. He crossed his arms, stomped his foot, and grinned at his successful attempt at copying Olivia. "Look, Sissy, I am just like you," Charlie said.

"No! Stop copying me, Charlie!" Olivia stamped her foot harder, throwing muddy water onto Charlie. He giggled and stomped in reply—the game ensued.

Frustrated, Olivia shoved Charlie and he pushed her back with a giggle that infuriates Olivia.

I decided that there will be no working out the conflict between the two of them, so I intervened before someone got hurt. "Olivia, let your brother play with you," I scolded her.

"But, Mommy. He's too little to be an elephant. You know that!" She rolled her eyes at me as if I had lost my mind with my request.

"He isn't much smaller than you. And besides, elephants love to be in a herd. They like their family."

"No," she stomped her foot again. "I remember Daddy said that the boy elephants have to leave the family when they get too big. It is the girl elephants and the babies that stay together."

I felt like I was about to lose an argument with my child once again. "Fine. Let Charlie be the baby elephant, and you can be the Momma," I reason.

"Fine." Olivia counters. "He can be an elephant with me, but this is my watering hole." Olivia pointed at the water and fisted her tiny hands to make her point more powerful.

Charlie copied her movements and tried to sneak into the pretend watering hole.

Olivia blocked his advance and, like a game of chess, she skillfully anticipated his movements and counters.

Charlie couldn't outsmart her, so he did the next best thing. He began to wail an ear piercing octave that I am sure could have shattered glass. It was time to intervene.

"Olivia, you know that elephants take turns sharing the water with their families. You have to share with Charlie."

"Mommy!" She pouted and kicked the ground in protest. "Why does Charlie have to ruin everything?" She yelled and stomped her foot again.

All the patience I tried to have slipped out of my hands and I was finished with Olivia's bossiness. "Olivia Jones. You come up here right now and sit beside me! You need to apologize to your brother and think about the way you are acting." I crossed my arms over my chest, so my stubborn child would know I was serious.

Olivia tramped up the porch steps dripping mud with each dramatic stomp of her foot against the five wooden steps. She plopped herself down beside me with a thud. Olivia grabbed her monkey, Jeena, and placed her on her shoulder. Jeena began to pick at Olivia's hair and it only agitated Olivia further. She batted at Jeena's hand, causing a high-pitched screech from the monkey who was now also splattered with mud from her furry-brown head to the tip of her long tail. Olivia stroked the monkey before placing her on the step next to her.

My husband, Matt walked around the side of the house just in time to see pouting Olivia place the monkey on the step. He had a small bouquet of wildflowers in his hand and a grin that caught my breath. Even though we have been married for many years, his smile still sends my pulse to quicken at the sight of those adorable dimples.

When Olivia noticed her father approaching, her face looked hopeful that she could charm her father like she always does when she is in trouble. She raised her arms for Matt to pick her up.

Matt looked from Olivia's face to mine and apparently decided to find out what caused me to punish our daughter. He momentarily fought the urge to scoop her up into his arms. "What's wrong with my little girl?" Matt said, handing me the bouquet.

Matt is blind to the fact that Olivia has successfully wrapped her father around her little finger since the day she came screaming into this world. This, of course, Matt denies, as any wrapped father would do in his place.

Olivia gave Matt a look of innocence. She shyly dropped her head; her long lashes and her curls falling to shield her face of sadness. "Daddy, I can never play alone. I don't want Charlie to always be with me. I wanna be an elephant by myself," she pouts. "It's not fair that he always has to be with me. I want to play alone like the leopards do."

I was impressed at how Olivia changed her argument to a lone animal to avoid the argument that elephants stay in a herd. Olivia is cunning in her game of chess that now countered me.

She continued to focus on her father. "Remember you told me that leopards don't like to be with their brothers and sisters? They go away from their family. That's why I shouldn't have to play with him." She pointed at her filthy, but grinning brother.

Matt walked to the bottom of the porch steps. He was unable to resist her and lifted Olivia into a hug, oblivious to the mud. She always plays on his sympathy with her big hazel eyes and the little curls on her head that tighten with the rain. "Mommy said that I have to sit on the porch, and now Charlie is having all of the fun. Can I go back to play, Daddy?" Olivia confidently played this mental game of chess like a pro.

Matt caught my gaze of frustration before answering Olivia's request. "Olivia, you have to do what your mother tells you to do. She will tell you when you can play again," he answered, placing her down on the step next to me.

Olivia smiled at me and tried to entice me with those dimples on her cheeks, which usually worked. But today, I was not going to cave. This chess game of wits has me having the next move. The game is not for the timid. I made my advance. "Remember what I asked you to do, Olivia?" I questioned sternly.

"Sit on the steps." Olivia countered.

"And what else?" I asked.

Olivia placed her pointer finger to her lips and looked skyward. "Uh, I can't remember."

"Oh, alright. You will sit here until you can tell me what it is that I've asked you to do."

"Err! Okay. I have to say sorry to Charlie." I mentally checked and felt as though I would win the game. "Well, you can go play with your brother after you do what I've asked you to do."

Olivia slid her bottom down the stairs and stood up in front of a messy Charlie, who was trying to shake mud from his dripping hands.

"Charlie, I am sorry that you are too little to be an elephant with me." Check mate. Olivia has done it again. She turned and gave me her biggest grin. Her clever ingenuity is abundant.

I looked over at Matt. He was grinning at Olivia's cleverness. "Well, she did what you asked," he laughed and leaned forward to twirl a piece of my hair that had fallen from my braid. "She did apologize. I like how you have streaks of light in your hair from the sun, Darling. It's the only sunny thing I've seen in a week." Matt gave my strand a playful tug.

He kissed my head. "Are you alright, Zura?"

"I need a break," I said, placing my hands in his. I want to go and speak with Momma. Are you in a place that you can take over the children?"

"Of course, Darling. You might also want to find out if your father is feeling alright. He looked more tired than usual today. He's not himself at all. He didn't even go with the men to bring back a baby that was spotted next to her dead mother's body." He became mournful. "Will the slaughter of elephants ever stop?"

"Not as long as men are in the jungle. It makes me wonder if the Tembo Project we started is even making a difference in stopping the killing."

"Zura, it helps. We have to believe that we can make a difference. Make sure you ask your mother about your father, alright?"

"It's probably all the rain that we've been getting. You know how he likes to go into the field and look for signs of sick and injured animals. It's been hard to do that in the storms. Maybe that's why he stayed behind."

"You are probably right. Just ask your mother to be sure."

"I will," I smiled up at Matt and he kissed me softly.

"That makes everything better," I laughed. "How did you make out today?"

"Your father and I took care of the new baby in the last pen. She looks like she may have been overly stressed. With some fluids and rest, she will be ready to be introduced to the rest of the herd in a few weeks. We will take it slow and have Neema be the first to see her. She has the best temperament. If Neema can welcome her, the rest will follow suit."

"Neema is a great choice. She has helped us welcome so many other injured and abandoned elephants over the years. She is a great girl. We are lucky to have her. It's too bad that the injury to her leg from the poacher's trap prevented us from giving her a life outside of the sanctuary. But she is a blessing. And she is safe."

Matt rubbed my arms. "Hopefully the herd outside of the sanctuary will welcome the new one into their group. Time will tell. What has Olivia decided to name her?"

"Oh, it's Maji."

"She named the baby elephant after water?"

"Well, you said the elephant needed water when she arrived, so Olivia thought it was a fitting name." I handed Matt the bouquet after taking in their scent.

"Clever girl. Go spend time with your mother. I will get the children cleaned up and start dinner. Don't worry, I will get your flowers into water." Matt gave me a hug and a kiss.

I start to walk down the well-worn path to my parent's home.

As I passed Tim and Isabella's house, I heard nothing but silence.

Isabella is a great mother. Her children are well mannered and always stay clean. Isabella's children never talk back and they do as they are told, which includes two-hour naps in the early afternoon. They are the direct opposite of my loud and rowdy children. Isabella's children would never play in the mud, and for that I felt sorry for them, never to know the mysteries of mud.

As I walked through the trees to my parent's home, the sun peeked through the clouds. It will not take long for the hot rays to dry up the earth once more. In the distance, another slow-moving storm was making its way over the mountains.

Before I had a chance to enter the home that I grew up in, I saw Momma standing on the side of the house. She was rubbing her arms and looking up at the sun.

Momma was wearing her *I am going to the field* outfit, complete with her tan pants, green button-down shirt, boots, and a large hat to keep the sun out of her eyes.

Momma never seems to age. Her eyes are still bright blue, her cheeks rosy and her skin barely shows a wrinkle. Momma carries herself like a queen. I often think it is because she was raised in the United States, before coming to Africa to start her life studying the elephants. She met my father and never left. When I was little, I would dream that she *was* a queen from a faraway place and I was a princess. I looked at her differently than I do as a grown woman.

Momma carried her well-worn bag that always contains her charting books. Her metal canteen was strapped to the back of the sack, along with a knife as a precautionary measure. I waved as she looked up in my direction. "Oh, you caught me just when I was heading to the field. My goodness, Zura. What is all over your legs? Is that mud?"

I looked down at my legs to find splashes of mud on my shins and knees. "Where else would you be going but the field?" I muttered to myself before I could stop it from coming out of my mouth.

"Olivia was being an elephant in a puddle of mud and splashed me before I left the house," I said, wiping at my legs and rubbing the dirt from my hands onto my tan shorts. Unsure of why my emotions were causing me to react negatively, I harnessed some good energy and joined Momma next to the house.

Momma gave me a quick hug and pulled me away to look at me. She wrinkled her nose in concern as she searched my eyes for an answer. "Zura, what's wrong? You look as though you are troubled by something. Is Charlie sick again?" Momma tucked the stray strand of hair behind my ear.

"Momma, I am fine. The children are fine," I answered unenthusiastically.

"Then what's wrong? Did you fight with Matt? Is there something wrong with that baby monkey that you are letting Olivia keep?"

"No, Matt is amazing. And the baby monkey is fine."

From the concerned look on Momma's face, I knew that she didn't like my answers. "Why don't you walk with me to the herd and we can talk," she suggested.

"Alright."

I took her trusty, worn bag, slung it over my shoulder and we walked to the field in silence. When we reached our ordinary spot under the shade of a rungu tree, Momma began to unpack her charts and books. She placed them on a blanket that she meticulously positioned under the tree.

I took in the view that never gets old. I like the peaceful vision of the moistened grass swaying in the warm breeze. In the distance, the zebra and antelope are eating the wet grass, lions shade themselves after a long night of hunting, and hyenas keep a close eye on the lions in hopes that they attack an animal and leave the leftovers. They always try to get a free meal. Hyenas are lazy poachers with a mean personality.

Momma placed her canteen on the blanket next to her and sat down beside me. She gazed off in the direction of the herd. The elephants were busy eating and rolling in the rich pools of mud from the recent storm.

"What's on your mind?" Momma asked, never taking her eyes off the elephant herd—except to write in her charts. "Will you look at that baby, she is so healthy and starting to show some spunk. She should be done nursing soon."

"I am not a good mother, I am not good at all," I blurted out.

Momma did not respond to my outburst. Her silence annoyed me. I seemed to have lost Momma's attention before we even started the conversation. I know that this is her routine, but just once, I wanted to feel as though I came first. Just once, I wish that she could put her work and the elephants' needs behind my own.

Talking louder, I startled the nearby herd of elephants. "I said I am not good, I am not a good mother!"

She doesn't flinch, even when she answers. "What do you mean you are not a good mother? You are a perfectly fine mother," she says with her nose in her book.

"Momma!" I yelled in frustration. "Can I please have your undivided attention for just a few minutes? I have spent my whole life fighting with the elephants for your attention. Surely you know that. Could you please put me first just once? I need to speak with you!"

Momma's face showed her dislike for my outburst. She slowly closed her book and placed it on her lap. Momma paused for a few seconds and let out a breath before she turned to address my mood.

"Alright Zura, let's talk about what has you so upset that you would lash out at me like that."

I lowered my gaze and began to shred a piece of the high grass, tearing it into strips to keep my hands busy. "I'm sorry, Momma. I am just so tired of feeling like nobody listens to me. Olivia constantly challenges me, Charlie is too little to understand, and Matt thinks that life is one big game. I can't get anyone to listen."

"I am listening, Zura. Why don't you get it all out? It will make you feel better." Momma's fingers drummed on her book.

I swallowed the unexpected large lump in my throat. I was about to reveal what I have been holding in for too long. "Alright," I took a deep cleansing breath. "I am not a good mother. Lord knows, I try to be. I love my children, I really do. My husband is amazing. We have a fine life together. I am not doing this right. I always knew that I would not be the kind of mother that my children deserve. Look at Isabella for instance. She has everyone in her home trained to listen to everything she wants them to do. Even Tim takes direction from her."

"Dear, Isabella doesn't work outside of the home. The running of the home, the raising of the children, that is her job. Are you saying that you want to stay at home more? Do you want to stop working with the elephants?"

"No, Matt and I have the perfect arrangement of who is with the children and who is working. That's not the issue. Momma, I love my time with the elephants and charting them. I get such a thrill when we can see them grow up. I am saying that I don't think I was meant to be a mother. I now understand why you were always missing from my life when I was young. It's why I had too much freedom and it's why…"

I couldn't finish my sentence and admit to my mother that on some deep level, way down deep, I blamed her for getting shot by the poachers that kidnapped me. If she would not have been in the field, she would have been in the way, and I wouldn't have fallen from the tree into captivity. It was too late to pull back what I already shared. I honestly did fault her for allowing me to roam in the jungle unattended and to climb trees that I had no business climbing. I blamed her. I never got over the fact that I ended up in the hands of killers. Men who held me captive; who died in the jungle. I led them into danger and watched them die, one by one. All except for Lonnie, who turned out to be very special to me. I held her responsible for allowing me to be free. I also blamed her for Tembo's death.

It was too late to take them back. The words continued to flow out of my mouth. "You have never let me talk about it! You never let me deal with what they put me through. Seeing death at such a young age, sleeping on the jungle floor surrounded by them, tied like a captured animal, and waiting for the next man to die. Let's not forget being hunted by a mad man who tried to kill me several times! It could have all been prevented if you were just a better..."

Momma stared blankly at me. My words stung like a thousand bees. It was there in her eyes. I could tell by the look on her face that I had said too much. "A better what? A better mother? Zura, you came home. You were safe."

Something inside of me burst. "Safe? Is that how you define safety? Because I was home? No Momma, I was not safe from the nightmares or the pain. I was terrified not knowing whether you were dead or alive. I was only eleven-years-old. Too young for all that death and terror. It did something to me. It made me afraid of the jungle that I love."

A movement and a sound caught my attention.

"Zura, how can you blame me?"

"Be quiet," I whispered and placed a finger to my lips.

Momma began to speak again until I touched her arm. "Something's wrong, Momma. Please, let me listen."

The sound of strangers who were too unaware of the dangers their voices would attract to their location reached me. I looked at the elephants. They perked and a few turned toward the noise. Others began to put more distance between them and the strangers.

The familiarity of the scenario took me instantly back to a time when the poachers entered the jungle. Back to the day I watched as Momma stood between her beloved elephants and the poachers and they shot her. That split second, many years ago, when I saw her fall and I fell right into captivity. It has been a nightmare that has haunted me all of my life and I just stepped back into it. Fear rattled my mind. My heart beat as if it would explode and my legs felt as though they would not be able to hold my weight if I stood.

"Zura, you are hurting my arm!" Momma whispered.

I realized that I was gripping her arm far too tightly, but I couldn't seem to let go.

My mind whirled with pictures of the past. If history repeats itself, because people are who they are, Momma will do whatever she can to protect her beloved elephants—even if she dies trying to save them.

I see her face change and know she has seen them too. She tried to stand. It was just like she did that day when I was too far away to save her. I was hanging on for dear life on a cracking limb in the tree. I could not reach her that day. But today is different. Today, I can stop her from making the same mistake again.

"No!" I yelled and pulled on her arm.

Momma cannot pull away from my grip. I threw my body on top of hers like a shield. A bullet ricocheted and pinged off the canteen. A second bullet collided into the dirt near my head. Dust wisped into the air in front of my face. All I can think of is protecting Momma.

I slid back into my nightmares, into the past that never really left. I fell into my own personal hell. Rolling to my side before sitting up I could see that look in her crazed eyes. It's a selfless plea. She grabs my arm "We have to stop them! They will kill my babies. Zura, we have to stop them!"

"Momma! We have to move! Come with me and crawl backward. You can do it. We have to get behind the tree. We need cover, quickly!"

"I can't leave them," Momma cried.

"You will!" I became unhinged. "I swear I'll drag you back! We have to save ourselves. Now, crawl back on all fours!" I instructed and tried to move as fast as possible while dragging Momma with me. She is too stunned to fight me and eventually moves on her own. The large tree sheltered us from another shot that rips its bark clean off.

Fear tingled up my spine and rested at the base of my neck. The hairs on my arms stood on end. In the pit of my stomach, the tension was building.

Hearing Momma's sobs and turning my attention to her, I whispered. "Momma, follow me, I will lead us through the jungle. There is a shortcut that will get us home."

Momma trembled but did as I instructed. As soon as we made it to the interior of the jungle, we ran faster than I ever thought we could. Momma struggled to keep the pace with me. She continued to run, probably out of an adrenaline rush, but mostly out of fear. She couldn't help herself from looking over her shoulder and back at the herd.

I slowed my pace to allow Momma to be by my side. We had a head start, if indeed anyone was chasing us.

We sprinted until Momma could run no further. She leaned forward and held her side, breathing heavily. "You go on," she insisted. "Leave me here. I'll catch my breath and then find my way home."

"Never. We both know what will happen. You will go right back to the herd. We will get out of here, even if I have to carry you. It's not much farther. Do you think you can make it, or can you climb on my back?"

"Don't be silly, I can make it," Momma snipped through heavy breaths. She glared at me as if I was the cause of all of this.

I slowed the pace even more for her sake, and led us through the deep underbrush, over downed trees, and around to the back side of Wild Hearts.

"Peter!" Momma yelled through her laboring breath. "Peter! Come quickly!"

Father responded to Momma's calls and opened the door that leads to his office. Utter panic showed on his face. "What? What's happened?" he asked, running toward the both of us with his hand on his chest.

Momma continued to breathe heavily. "Men," she says through large gasps for air. "Men. They were in the jungle. They are trying to shoot the elephants. We have to go back!"

Father looked from Momma to me, his eyes wide with the realization that history was now the present.

"I would not let her stand this time," I said.

Father nodded in agreement. "Zura, take your mother to your house. Tim and I will go and check out the field. Afterwards, we will all sit down to discuss this."

I started to help Momma down the path that leads to my home. She was sniffing back tears and wiping her tears with the back of her hand.

My brother, Tim came running down the hill from his home.

"I heard some yelling. Tim reached us and put an arm around Momma to help me guide her. She leaned on Tim and away from me. Tim stroked her arm. The same arm that I gripped so hard it was now beginning to bruise. "Are you both alright? What happened?" Tim questioned.

Father joined us on the path. He was carrying his rifle and started to haphazardly load it. His hands were shaking and all of the color was drained from his face. Father placed his arm around my waist and looked at Tim.

"Let's get them into Zura's house first and then you and I should check the field."

When we reached the top of the hill, I saw Matt standing at the screen door of our home. He had a squirming Charlie in his arms and Olivia hanging onto his leg. Matt put Charlie down when he saw the four of us rushing toward the porch. "Olivia, be nice to your brother," he stated loud enough for all to hear. Matt opened the screen door and rushed to us. He grabbed both sides of my face and looked worriedly into my eyes. "What's happened? You look as though you have seen a ghost."

"Maybe I have," I answered.

"Come on, let's get the two of you inside," Matt said. Worriment was causing his eyebrows to pinch together. "Zura, you are scaring me. What's happened?" He looked me over from head to toe for any sign of injuries.

I placed my hand on Matt's cheek to settle him. "I am alright. We are both okay."

Momma was visibly shaken. She looked at me as if she was broken. I wonder if she too is thinking of the past. I would like to think the look was a mother who worries about her child. I imagined it must have been horrible for her to wonder and wait for news of me when I was in the hands of the poachers. Still, I wondered if the reason she never wanted to talk about it was because I was taken or because an elephant had almost died.

I looked at Olivia and Charlie. They were peeking out of the door trying to see what all of the fuss was about. As a mother, I know I have to look at it from Momma's perspective and what it would do to me if one of my children were missing. It would destroy me.

Tim helped Momma into the house and to a seat at the kitchen table. When I sat down beside her, we stared at each other. Her eyes filled with sadness and worriment that went beyond her elephants. A mother's eyes overflowing with tears. I can only hang my head in shame at the feelings that I shared with her in the field. I never considered that guilt and fear of losing me caused her to never want to talk about the time she almost lost me.

Father's concern for her showed on his face and he gently brushed away her tears. "There, there, Rosie. It's alright. No one is going to hurt your herd of elephants. We will see to it."

Momma dried her face with the folded napkin from the dinner setting. "I'm alright," she said, looking at me as if I had broken her heart.

Matt placed some meat and bread with honey on the table beside me. "Why don't the two of you have some food? It will help you to eat something," he said.

I had too much adrenaline pulsing through my body to sit still. So I stood and began to pace. I can't take the words back that I said to Momma. I can't erase the feelings that festered inside of me for so long. The painfully suppressed memories came back in a swarm of emotions. My mind jarred with each hit from the past. I remembered as if it was yesterday. The monsters from my dreams as a child were based on those men. Bain and Uncle's cruelty. Jasper, Curtis, and Otis died unnecessarily and were left for the animals to consume. I had tried to bury it to make my parents feel better. I repressed the echoes of the pain deep underground. And today, they rose to the surface to meet me in the same spot, the same field that started the terror all those years ago. A group of men shooting at the herd. Momma trying to stand to protect her treasured elephants. But this time was different. This time I was able to protect her and to pull her down onto the ground instead of watching her take a bullet. My actions probably saved both of our lives.

The mindless thoughts reverberated in my head. Why was I thinking that I had just saved us? Why were the shots even close to us? The herd was not that close for the bullets to be landing near my head.

Father's voice brought me back to the present. "Now, Zura, can you please have a seat with the rest of us?"

"Momma, can I make you some tea?" Without waiting for an answer, I began heating water to make tea for the both of us.

Father gave me the few minutes that I needed to compose myself before I joined my family around the table.

We sat in our family circle. The men anxiously waited until we took a few sips before they began interrogating Momma and me. All three of them started barreling questions at us so fast, we didn't know how to answer.

Momma closed her eyes and raised her finger to her lips to shush them. She calms the household. "Let me tell you what happened first, and then if you still have questions, we will try to answer them. Alright?"

The men nodded in unison and the room was silent as Momma began the explanation. "Zura and I were talking, and we both saw movement by the tree line. We saw that there were men, and I wanted to get up to stop them from poaching one of my dear elephants, but Zura threw herself on top of me. We crawled back behind a tree and then we ran into the jungle to make it back home."

Father stood and began to pace the room. "Did they look familiar?" Father placed a protective hand on Momma's shoulder. He directed the question toward me.

Momma and I answered at the same time. A definite yes and a no are left hanging in the air. I say yes, and Momma says no. I am not sure why I answered the question with a yes. I tried to correct my original thought. "I didn't recognize them. They were pretty far away to get a good look at their faces."

My brother, Tim, scowled at me. "Why did you say yes?"

"I don't know."

"You don't know why you said it, or you don't know them?"

I paused and looked around the room. "I don't know why I said it. There is no way that I could have known them."

Tim and I stared at each other for a long moment. He is the only other person that knows exactly what I went through, because that is where we met. His only living relative, Warren, was the ringleader of the poachers. Warren's plan was to lose or kill Tim in the jungle. That's when I made the decision to try to save Tim and myself.

Father began to take charge again. "Matt, you and I will search the area. Get your gun for protection. Tim, do you want to get Isabella and the children and come back here? We should keep the whole family together while we sort this out."

Tim nodded and looked at me. "I am already thinking the same thing. It won't take us long, Zura. We will be back shortly, alright? Don't worry, Isabella will help keep the children in line. She is an amazing mother."

I sink a little lower in my chair. Momma and I shared a glance. She now knows that I feel inferior to Isabella's talents as a mother.

Momma is a great diverter and she stood to address the men. "Please grab my things, alright? I left all of my work in the field on the blanket," Momma announced.

I sighed loudly and addressed the men. "We will be fine. Momma and I will stay here and feed the children. We will get them ready for bed." I turned toward Matt, who was grabbing ammunition from the high shelf over the stove. "Can I have a moment, Matt?"

"I will be back soon, my love," he said and turned to kiss me on the head. He ran out of the door before I could speak to him. My attention was diverted with the sound of Charlie and Olivia miraculously playing with each other in the living room.

I peeked around the corner to see Olivia covering Charlie with a blanket. Charlie was pretending to be asleep with a huge grin on his face.

"Olivia, I am very proud of you for playing with your brother."

"Oh, I am the mommy. Charlie and Jeena are my babies," she says, uncovering the monkey to show me. Jeena's tail snakes out from the blanket and she wraps it around Olivia's arm.

"Come have something to eat, both of you," I called to my children.

They both ran to the table to eat.

Olivia placed Jeena on the table.

I gave Olivia a stern look. "No monkeys on the table."

"But Mommy, my baby has to eat too," Olivia protests.

"Put her on the chair next to you, Olivia. You can feed her there."

Olivia pulled several plant shoots from inside of her blanket and placed them on the table next to her. Jeena had another plan. She grabbed two wildflowers from the arrangement in the middle of my table and began to eat them.

"Olivia, off the table, now!" I lost my temper.

Olivia placed Jeena on the seat next to hers and coddled the monkey as Jeena greedily ate my flowers.

The children ate quickly and wanted to go back to playing. I cleaned them and put them in their night clothes before I allowed them to play.

I looked in on them when I heard shouting. Olivia is telling Charlie to sit down. "I told you to do it!" She yelled. "Do it now!"

Knowing that Olivia is repeating my angry tone, I shrank into the chair across from Momma and sipped on my cold tea. I silently looked down into my murky cup. The weight of the day felt like it was smothering me.

Momma cleared her throat and unconsciously stirred her tea. "You must hate me. You must hate me for being a terrible mother."

I sighed. "I don't hate you."

"I wouldn't blame you if you did. I have been a horrible mother to you. I wasn't there for you, always focusing on my own selfish needs." Momma began to cry again. She wiped her tears on her sleeve. You were going to say that if I would have been paying attention, you wouldn't have gone through what you did many years ago. Am I right?"

"Yes, that's what I said, but I was wrong. Momma, you are a wonderful mother and grandmother. We love you very much."

"But when you were little."

"When I was little, I couldn't deal with what I had been through."

"And can you now? I can see it in your face, Zura. You are not sharing your thoughts. You are terrified sometimes. You don't sleep well and have those nightmares all of the time."

I don't know how to respond. I struggle with trying to decipher my feelings, trying to process the events of the day and separate the past from the present. There was something else that was nagging at me, beyond the riff that I caused between Momma and me. Something that bothered me about the men we encountered. I wasn't sure that Momma and I shared the same feelings about the men in the jungle. I was leaning toward something more sinister.

Tim, Isabella, and their children arrived before my father and Matt came back from the field. It wasn't long before we all sat around my kitchen table again.

Isabella stood when she heard a ruckus in the living room between Olivia and her cousin, Little Peter. "I will take care of the children," she said, taking my hand and kissing my head. Can I borrow some blankets and pillows and set the children to sleep in the living room? I have a feeling this conversation may last a long time."

"Of course, you can. Do you know where they are?"

"Yes, I can manage. You just sit here and try to calm your nerves, Zura. Everything is under control."

The snakehead of jealousy slithered into me, knowing that Isabella's skills as a mother far outweigh my own. It wasn't the time for self-pity, so I brought my concentration back to the worried family sitting around the table.

Father's impatience showed. He stood and began to pace again around the kitchen. "I can't believe that these poachers think that they can get away with this. Luckily, whomever was the shooter was a bad shot. None of the elephants have been harmed. That is good news."

Momma raised her hand to her heart. "Oh, thank goodness. Isn't that wonderful news, Zura?"

"Yes, it is Momma," I answered, deep in my own thoughts. Now that they are forming, I am afraid to share them.

Tim took a sip of tea and winked at me. "We should set up a watch around the elephants and in a few days, they will realize that they cannot get to the elephants and they will leave."

Matt rubbed my back and kissed the side of my head. "That's a splendid idea. We can take turns watching. There are three of us that can divide the time in the field. We can be sure that they will not try to kill them at night. Who would be out in the bush when the big cats are hunting? We take a watch from daybreak until dusk. We will rotate every two hours, so that we can each still get our work accomplished, even if it is only for a few days."

The men had it all figured out. They ran through their plans for several hours. The men in our family take charge; they have all the answers. Father led the planning with his authoritative voice on ammunition, supplies, rifles, and how the shifts will rotate.

I sat in silence, self-absorbed in my own thoughts, knowing Momma is staring at me. I can't help but avoid her gaze out of guilt. My words hurt her, and she will be obsessing over how to make amends for things that happened so long ago. Truth be told, I felt as though I ended up just like her. Spending endless hours working on the Tembo Project, trying to get the message about poaching and creating an awareness all over the world. I even did an interview for an important newspaper in the United States. I was so deep into my own project, that my children were not getting my full attention.

"Zura. Zura! Can you answer my question, please?" Father scolded and rubbed at his left arm.

"Oh, I am sorry. I guess I was not paying attention. A lot on my mind. What was the question again?"

My father is usually a patient person, but with his family and the herd in potential danger, he was on edge. And yet, I instinctively know that there is something else going on. I see it in my mother's eyes. It's a worry for my father.

Momma searches my father's face. "Peter. Please sit down."

"I am alright," he snaps. My father never raises his voice at Momma, and I am even more suspicious.

Father stops pacing when he makes eye contact with Momma again. "Please pay attention," he directs his comment at me but lowers his voice. "Alright, Zura? Is there anything else that you can remember about the men that would help us to recognize them, and not mistake tourists that occasionally come our way?"

Tim chimes in. "Remember that the gentleman who represents an investor from the United States, he and his crew will be coming this week to talk about taking the Tembo Project global."

"Yes, I remember," Father answered. "Let's not mistake them for the poachers in the jungle, alright? Zura, what about you, anything familiar about them?"

"Like I said earlier, they were too far away for me to see them up close."

Tim spoke to the group but watched me carefully. "As I was saying. The investor's representative. I heard from the university in Chicago. We do have several visitors coming in from the United States. There are three men and a woman that will be camping close by. Let's not mistake them for poachers, alright? They represent folks interested in getting involved with the Tembo Project after seeing the article about Zura in the Chicago News. They are considering helping us to expand our activist audience. We have to make a very good impression. Shooting one of them would definitely not be a great idea."

"That's fantastic news!" Momma whispered. "Zura, aren't you excited?"

"That is good news. It's a good opportunity to add to our supporting base."

Tim beamed. "It's going to be big. I'll give you a copy to read. The pictures turned out amazing. And it was very brave of you, Little Sister, to talk about our past with the gentleman from the newspaper."

"Let's not make a habit of me doing interviews. You know I am not good with strangers. They make me nervous and angry. That guy knew nothing about elephants and what we go through."

Tim smiled. "Well, that is the purpose of the interview, Sister. To learn about our ways, the plight of the elephants and draw awareness."

"You do the interview next time. You know everything I know." I lied to get out of any more appearances.

"You don't think I know when you are lying, Zura?" Tim said, seeing right through me.

I hung my head. That was the last thing I wanted to think about after the day's events. No more poachers, no more killing, I couldn't take it. Yet, when I saw the men, something was familiar. Maybe it was the scene. I couldn't put my finger on it just then.

Matt looked at me and interjected. "I think this has been enough activity for today. We should let the children sleep. Let's call it a night, alright? I think Zura is tired."

I smiled meekly at Matt and nodded.

Tim rose and gave Momma a hug. "Isabella and I will sleep in the spare bedroom here, if that is alright with my sleepy sister."

"It's alright, of course," I answered. I didn't even want to get into the fact that I wasn't sleepy. In fact, I was sure that I would not get any sleep because the thoughts in my brain were still gnawing at me. Something was troubling me about the whole thing.

Momma and Father rose to get ready to go home. Momma's hug was longer and harder than usual, like she was afraid to let go.

I whispered in her ear. "It's alright, Momma. I love you," I said for only her ears to hear.

Momma silently wiped away a tear and turned to leave. "Let's go home, Peter, I am very tired," Momma said without looking back.

I sat at the table, holding my head in my hands. A painful headache was creeping its way from the back of my neck and making itself at home above my eyes. I rubbed my head and tried to take deep breaths to sooth my nerves.

Matt stood behind me and rubbed my neck and shoulders. "This was a stressful day for you. Why don't you go upstairs and rest?"

"I am not tired, just stressed from all the activity today."

Tim wrapped an arm around Isabella as she rubbed at her belly. It's not a stomach ache that had her rubbing. It's a baby. I decided to let her tell me when she is ready. She probably doesn't want to put one more thing out there for me to absorb, though I would welcome the distraction.

Tim sat forward, his eyes excitedly dancing. "I can't wait to meet the travelers. It's been some time since I have seen someone from the States, except for that person that came to do the interview about Zura and Wild Hearts. Aren't you excited, Zura?"

"Why would I be excited?"

"Well, because it's a chance to meet new people. Maybe make a friend from far away."

"I have all the friends I need. I have family, the elephants, and an occasional scientist that comes to see the wildlife, not someone poking into my life."

Tim chuckled. "There, there, Sister. You sound a little bitter."

I forced a smile at Tim. "I guess I do. You know I don't do well with strangers. They usually end up staring at me."

Matt laughed from behind me. "Maybe it's because you are so tall for a woman. Ever think of that?" Matt kissed my cheek.

Tim stood and put a hand out to Isabella. She stood with a toss of her hair, her blonde curls dance on her shoulders and she was glowing. "I am getting tired. I will see you in the morning, Zura."

Isabella circled the table and leaned forward to hug me. "We will talk about what happened between you and Momma tomorrow, alright?"

"Alright," I said. "Thanks for everything, Izzy."

She nodded and smiled. "Good night," Isabella yawned.

Tim and Isabella checked on the children then retired to the spare bedroom.

Matt reached for my hand and pulled me to my feet. "Let's go to bed."

He swung me into a hug and gently swayed me into a slow dance. I pulled away to look into his hazel eyes. Flecks of yellow, like the grasses in the field disappeared under his heavy eyelids and long lashes.

Matt and I went upstairs to our room to get ready for bed. He sat on the edge of the bed, watching me brush and silently plait my long hair.

"You are very quiet tonight, my dear."

"I'm alright." I shrugged.

"Do you want to tell me what's bothering you? Have I done something to upset you?"

I stopped looking at myself in the mirror, and turned toward Matt. "Of course not. I just have a lot on my mind."

"More than what happened in the field today? More than the almost shooting of one of the elephants?"

"That's the thing. I can't put my finger on it, but something about it doesn't feel right."

"Of course, it doesn't feel right. Any time men go into the jungle to kill a wild animal, it doesn't feel right."

"It's more than that."

"Tell me, Zura. Start telling me and maybe you will figure it out." Matt moved to the middle of the bed.

"Alright. Suppose you were with a group of men and you were going to poach an animal."

"I'd never do that."

"I know you would never do that but stay with me." I stood and went to my side of the bed and adjusted my pillow. I sat on top of the covering to face Matt.

Matt turned to look at me with deep concern on his face. "Alright, I am with a group of men and we are going to poach an animal."

"So, do you use the person that is the best shot, or the worst shot?"

"That's a silly question. I use the person who is the best shot, of course."

"Exactly!"

"Okay, how is that relevant?" Matthew asked.

"The best shot could have taken any one of those elephants. But they didn't. They missed at least three or four times. What if they were not aiming for the elephants? What if the elephants were not the target?"

"What other animals were in the field? Maybe they wanted another species."

I paused to reflect on the other animals that may have been present in the field. "There were some zebras."

Matt raised a hand. "There you go. They were poaching a zebra."

"Again, why would you use your worst shooter to kill a zebra? You wouldn't." I stood and began to pace around the room. My hands clenched in worry and my head was overcome with too many thoughts at one time. "What am I missing? What am I missing?" I began to chant. "Why can't I piece it all together," I mumbled to myself.

"Zura," Matt said in a calming voice. "You have to slow down. You are getting yourself into hysterics. What are you getting at?"

"I don't know. It's just an idea that has been bothering me all day."

Suddenly, it hit me like a full-grown rhino running at full speed and I sat back down on the bed. "It's me."

"You? What do you mean, it's you?" Matt grabbed my shoulders to turn me toward him. "That's ridiculous, Zura. Nobody is shooting at you."

"They were aiming at me, it's clear to me now."

"Zura, don't be absurd. Listen to me, nobody is aiming at you. Who would want to hurt you? You are one of the most caring and giving people on the planet. Nobody is after you. I think the whole thing with your mother trying to stand, and you throwing yourself on top of her, brought back some bad memories. That's all it is. Being in the wrong place at the wrong time. I don't like to see you worry yourself like this," he said, reaching over and rubbing my arm. "Get some rest, and I think you will feel differently in the morning when you've had some sleep."

I decided that it is probably better for everyone if I keep these thoughts to myself. Not one of my family will be able to handle my theory that someone wants me dead.

I was barely asleep when I felt a light touch on my arm that made me sit straight up in bed. I gasped for air before my eyes could adjust. It was Isabella standing at the side of my bed. She bent down to whisper in my ear, so as to not wake Matt. "I am sorry to startle you, Zura.

I can't find Olivia. I went downstairs to check on the children one last time before bed and I noticed that she's not with the other children. I thought that maybe she came up here to her own bed and when she wasn't there either, I thought maybe she was with you."

"It's alright. I will get her."

"Get her? You know where she is?"

"Yes, Izzy. Come with me. I will show you what I have been dealing with. Maybe you can give me some advice, since I am obviously failing at motherhood."

"Oh, Zura. Why would you say such a thing? You are a fine mother." Isabella laid her hand on my arm.

I grabbed my shawl, my shoes, and my 642 Swiss and Wesson .38 Special. It was a gift from Matt and it came with a promise that I would carry it with me when I was alone in the jungle. Because it was the middle of the night, I thought it appropriate to have some protection for Isabella and myself.

Isabella followed me down the stairs and out onto the porch. We stopped for a moment so that I could slip into my shoes and load my gun. "I have been doubting my abilities lately, and this just confirms that I do not have control over my children when they do things like this. She has been doing this ever since I allowed her to keep the orphaned vervet. That little monkey just lost its mother and clings to Olivia every chance she gets. Why, I even caught Olivia putting one of Charlies' shirts on the monkey. Olivia wraps it in a blanket and carries it all over the place. I am usually alright with it during the day, but I thought that maybe it should sleep out with the other animals at night. I will show you why this has become impossible."

With only the light of Isabella's candle to light the way, we walked to the back of the house and up the slight hill to the little barn that Matt and Tim built during the dry season. I lifted the wooden latch and opened the squeaky barn door. We entered the barn to find one of our newest elephants, Maji, sleeping in the first pen. In the second pen, on top of the dried grasses that we store as bedding for the animals, was Olivia. She was snuggled up with her little vervet monkey, Jeena.

I see that Olivia managed to cover herself with Jeena held tightly to her chest. Jeena's long tail was visible as it wrapped around Olivia's arm.

Isabella looked at me with great concern. "She is coming out here on her own? In the middle of the night?" Isabella whispered and moved Jeena to allow me to carry Olivia back to the house.

"Yes, almost every night. See now why I am a bad mother? I can't get her to stop. Olivia is stubborn and does whatever she wants."

Isabella's silence was all the confirmation that I needed. My mothering talents were an epic fail.

Olivia stirred from the movement of being carried back toward the house. "Mommy, is it morning time?"

"No, Olivia. It is not morning," I said sternly. "You and I will be having another talk about why you cannot leave the house to sleep in the barn. You know what the rules are, Olivia. Mommy is very disappointed in you. If you continue this behavior, you will not be allowed to keep Jeena."

"But Mommy! Jeena is all alone. She doesn't have her Mommy to tuck her in, and to read her a story. She needs to be with someone. She is sad. When you were little, didn't you ever want your Mommy when you were all alone?"

I stopped dead in my tracks and looked down at a sleepy Olivia. She cannot know just how much I needed my mother when I was young. How much I still need her. A sudden rush of guilt swept over me. I said some things to my mother that I should never have said. I knew that I had to find Momma first thing in the morning and apologize to her.

I tucked Olivia in before I went back to bed. She fell back to sleep as I stroked her hair.

Quietly, I made my way to my bedroom and tried not to disturb Matt when I pulled back the light covers and slipped into bed. Matt did not stir. He was always a sound sleeper. I am envious of his ability to put aside everything and rest easily.

Exhausted, I fell asleep quickly, only to be dragged down into the depths of my nightmares. I dreamed that I was standing on the edge of Thinking Rock. *Bain, with his scarred and scary enraged face, is so mad that he shoots. The bullet hits me in the shoulder. Blinding pain causes me to drop to my knees and cry out in agony. In a quick second, Bain's body turns into a gigantic Black Mamba. He slithers closer and closer, hissing and showing his enormous fangs. I am on the edge of Thinking Rock with no-where to go. He lunges at me as I fall from the rocks.*

The dream shifts, and I am now located in the cave behind the waterfall. My favorite hiding place, the place that I hid Tim when we were being hunted by Bain.

A fire is burning near the entrance of the cave. The water flows swiftly and dangerously in front of its opening.

I turn to see a dark shadow coming closer. As the shadow enters the light, I am terrified to see a male lion standing in front of me. He has the same scars as Bain running rigidly down his face. The lion's reverberating roar brings me to my knees. His sharp claws slice through my body and he tears my flesh from my bones. I do the only thing I can. I roll myself off the ledge and into the cool water.

I am falling for what feels like minutes. The rocks below grow closer and closer in my descent.

I hear the scream coming from the opening of the cave. "Jaaaane! Jaaaane! I will find you and kill you, Jaaaane!"

I woke up with a jolt! Covered in sweat, I felt Matt gently trying to shake me.

"Zura, that nightmare has to be one of the worst that I have ever seen. You tossed and turned and screamed."

I caught my breath and tried to slow my rapid heartbeat before I faced Matt.

"Whew." I wiped the sweat from my brow and turned toward him. "That was intense."

"Do you want to talk about it?"

"No."

"I could have guessed that that would be your answer. You never want to talk about it."

"It's just a dream, Matt. There is nothing to talk about. I'm fine."

"You are not fine. I can only imagine the nightmares that anyone would have, going through what you did as a child. Sweetheart, the bad men are dead. They cannot hurt you any longer."

"I guess the event of today took me back to that time and place. I know you are right."

Matt kissed my head and cuddled in close. "Try to get some sleep, alright?"

"Yes, you too. Sorry I woke you. Good night," I said and turned on my side to face away from Matt.

The tumultuous thoughts could not be tamed. I had been lying awake for hours, unable to settle my mind. As I tossed and turned in bed, Matt woke again and rolled toward me. "Dear, what is the matter? Can't you sleep? I know you well enough to know that you are stewing over the nightmare and the events of the day. You have to just stop thinking about it all and get some rest."

"Easy for you to say."

"Zura, please try."

Of course, you are right, Matt. I will try. I am sorry that I woke you," I said and kissed his cheek.

Within a few minutes, Matt was back to snoring, so I knew that it was safe to ignore his advice and go downstairs. Trying to be careful not to wake the children in the living room but wanting to make sure that Olivia was asleep with her cousins, I tip-toed into the room. As I was glancing away, a long tail caught my attention. It peeked out of the blanket that was wrapped around Olivia. Olivia has successfully left again. She went to the barn and brought Jeena into the house. I should have been furious that she disobeyed me again. In truth I was too exhausted to sleep, or to care about the monkey. I caught myself repeating what I had heard my mother say earlier in the day; *she was home, she was safe.*

I now understood that line of reasoning in a mother's mind. It was much safer to give her the monkey than have her roaming around outside in the middle of the night.

I decided on some tea to help me relax.

Weekly, I use a hammer to wilt the leaves. Then I ferment and dry them out. Momma says that Rooibos reminds her of caramel. The taste is not bitter like other black teas. It's my favorite.

I slipped out the door to sit on the porch steps and sip on the steaming tea. The moon was almost full, causing light and shadows in the trees. My imagination allowed me to see some ominous shapes that caused me to be fearful.

I went back inside the house and sat at the well-worn, wooden kitchen table. It was too early to make breakfast, too early to do anything but sit and remain a prisoner of my thoughts.

I usually do not doubt my gut, and it was telling me that whomever was in the jungle wasn't aiming for the elephants. But why? Why would there be someone out there that hated me so much that they wanted to kill me? There was no one alive that felt that way toward me. At least I didn't think there was anyone. My circle of family and acquaintances is small. That's the way I like it.

With my tea gone, I poured some water from the pitcher on the table and inhaled a large amount of it. Placing the cup down, I noticed that Tim left the newspapers from the United States in a pile on my table. The first paper was opened to the article about me as a child and my family today. I hesitated to pick it up when I saw Tembo's deformed ear almost at the crease in the paper. I pulled the paper in front of me on the table. There I was, in a black and white photo, standing next to Tembo whose trunk was rubbing in my hair. I posed for a lot of pictures and remembered that it was a wondrous day of playing with Tembo and swimming on his back in the river. It was right before my mother decided that we should try to introduce Tembo to the new herd that settled close by.

There was a recent photograph of Olivia and Charlie on the back of Little Maji, the baby elephant that was rescued a few months earlier. And another photograph of Matt, me, and our children, with Tim and his family.

The one that twisted my heart though was the one of me riding Tembo with Cha-cha, my ever-faithful wild dog that was draped in front of me over Tembo's back. His black, tan and white coat was unusual. His ears were extremely big, and his loyalty took down Bain, who tried to kill me.

I knew the picture to have been taken shortly after I escaped the kidnapping and torture, and right after Tim left with Lonnie to return to the United States.

There was another picture of Tim and me when we were playing in the rain. I was dancing around, and he was trying to avoid the mud that my feet were flinging in his direction. I had to smile over the bond that I had, and still have, with an orphaned boy in the jungle who became my brother through the terror. Our bond is every bit as strong as a true brother and sister.

That picture reminded me of my own daughter and son who love to play in the mud. I smiled, remembering Olivia trying to be an elephant yesterday, doing the same thing that I did when I was young.

I have to admit that telling the story about when I was captive, and Tim and I escaping Tim's evil uncle, is a difficult story to tell. Those memories of the hit man Bain chasing us, shooting at me and him being killed by Tembo stomping him to death, seems like it was just yesterday. I could still hear the cracking and grinding of his skull being crushed. It probably contributed to my recent feelings about my mother's parenting skills.

My memories have not faded. Momma's inability to let me talk freely about what had happened probably contributed to the fact that I can't stop remembering the past. It's always with me; not only in my sleep. It's there even when I am awake and distracted. It always sits there waiting for me to jump at a sudden sound.

It's led me to be an overprotective mother when it comes to Olivia's desire to explore the jungle. I won't even let her climb a tree. It's too hard for me to see her doing the things that landed me into my nightmares.

It was even more difficult to talk about when Tembo was slaughtered for his tusks and how I fell apart. But he was the reason that the Tembo Project exists. Having recognition from the United States was sure to help our cause. That had to be my only focus.

My eyes scanned to the top of the article and I didn't like the title: "They Called Her Jane". I never wanted to be reminded of the tormenting way that Bain called out to me before he tried to kill me, and I wished that Tim had not shared that with the reporter writing the article.

The picture at the bottom of the article was an old photograph of me at the age of eleven. I was skinny with messy hair and dirt all over my shorts. Cha-cha was standing by my side. He was looking up at me with those keen hunter eyes. Cha-cha's loyalty never wavered, even on the day he died, he sought me out and crawled into my lap to take his last breath.

On the other side of me was my beloved elephant, Tembo. His trunk was in my hair; a gesture that he did whenever he saw me. Father said that it was like a handshake. I liked to think that it was more like an elephant hug. Those beautiful tusks were still growing, but how brilliant they were. Of course, they were the reason that he was poached, something I never quite got over. How I missed my treasured Tembo and my faithful dog, Cha-cha. Thoughts of them made me think about how I was not allowing Olivia to fully enjoy her baby Jeena. Monkeys are highly social animals and it probably made sense that Jeena needed to feel protected at night. If I was to be honest with myself, I would admit that I didn't want Olivia to feel the same hurt that I continue to feel over the passing of my beloved animals. Time does not heal everything.

The sun was starting to rise, so I ventured back out onto the porch to sit in my usual spot on the top step. I opened the newspaper and found interesting articles about how to make a perfect pie crust, the newest rage in makeup, and a large picture of a woman with what looked like light, curly, short hair. Her lips looked painted. Her eyelashes were extremely long. Makeup looks like a mask to me. It hides the natural beauty of women.

I ran my fingers through my long, thick, earth-colored hair. I couldn't remember when I last cut the ends of my hair. The article said every eight weeks was the time for a trim. I ran my hands over my face and wondered whether Matt missed seeing a woman who paints her face with makeup.

I was so focused on my thoughts and life in the United States, I lost track of the time.

I folded the newspaper article about my life and the hair and makeup article to slip them into my shorts. When I heard the squeak of the screened door opening, I turned to see Isabella coming out onto the porch. She looked well-rested and happy, just like she always does at any time of the day. Her hand was on her belly.

I have seen her have that look before. It was impending motherhood. It wasn't anything that she says; more like what she does. Like how she absentmindedly rubs her belly before she takes a seat next to me on the steps. She is eating a piece of bread, which means her stomach is queasy. These are small things that a woman notices about another woman; a sister will see in her sister.

"Zura, how long have you been out here?" Isabella questioned and took a bite of her bread.

"I am not sure."

"You have to rest, Sister."

"Apparently, so do you, Sister," I countered and smiled at her.

"Meaning?"

"Meaning, does Momma and Father know that they will be grandparents yet again?"

"Did Tim tell you? It was meant to wait until we figure out what is going on with the poachers in the jungle. I would never want to take the attention away from something so important to you and Momma."

"Izzy, this family could use a diversion. Some happy news may be just what Momma needs to settle her nerves. Don't you think? And no, Tim did not tell me. I just knew".

"I suppose you are right. Would you like to go with me this morning to tell her together?"

"I would love to. I have some apologizing to do to Momma anyway."

"Apologizing? What did you do?"

"I called her out on my childhood and her lack of attention to my needs just before the shooting started yesterday. I hurt her, Izzy. And I have to make it right."

Isabella placed her tiny, delicate hand on top of my own. "We will go together. You apologize and then I will tell her my news so that we can distract her."

"I like the way you think, Sister," I said and hugged her before rubbing her slightly protruding belly. "Boy or girl? What are your thoughts?"

"Oh, I think it is a boy."

"What tells you that it is a boy?"

"I had the same amount of nausea with Little Peter."

"Since you named your first son after Father, do you think you will name this one after Tim?"

"We haven't had that discussion yet, I think we will wait until the time gets closer before we make that decision. Let's go and have some coffee," Isabella says, rising and putting out a hand to help me to stand.

When the sun started to come up over the trees, the children began to stir. Isabella made herself some tea and I drank my second cup of coffee. She prepared eggs for our hungry broods. I sliced the bread and poured some honey into a small bowl and placed it on the table.

The creaking of the floorboards above our heads told me that our men were up and walking about upstairs.

Tim's footsteps clamored slowly down the stairs and he joined us in the kitchen. He stood behind Isabella and rubbed his eyes that still wanted to sleep. "Coffee, I need coffee, woman," he said patting Isabella on the backside and kissing her cheek. She giggled, and her blonde curls bounced in delight.

Matt came down the stairs adjusting his suspenders. He scooped me up for a big kiss as the children came into the kitchen screaming. Olivia was the loudest as she fought with her cousin, Little Peter.

Little Peter is eight years old and does not like her bossy ways. "Stop telling me what to do, Olivia. You are not my mom," Peter said and nudged her away from himself.

"Hey! Don't push me. That wasn't nice," Olivia shouted.

Kara and Cora, walked behind their older cousins with Charlie between them. They held his hands to spin and dance with him. Their little handmade dresses billowed out in a beautiful display. The three were happy cousins that enjoyed their time together.

I remembered when Olivia and Little Peter were just as close. Now that they are getting older, Little Peter feels too old to play with Olivia, and Olivia feels that way about the twins and Charlie, leaving Olivia without a playmate. Another reason why she gravitates toward the animals.

The bickering between Olivia and Little Peter continued. I allowed them to try to work out their differences, so I was willing to stay quiet unless it got out of hand.

Isabella, however, had a different feeling about it and took charge. "Both of you sit on opposite sides of the table. You will have to look at each other through breakfast, so that hopefully you will remember that you are family, and family needs to stick together."

Olivia and Little Peter quietly took their seats and glared at each other. Without even turning around, Isabella called them out on their actions. "And I don't want to see any more faces made at each other. Do we understand one another?"

"Yes, Auntie Izzy," Olivia said and hung her head.

"Yes, Ma'am," answered Little Peter. "How did she do that?" Little Peter whispers to Olivia.

"I don't know. She wasn't even looking at us. Maybe she has eyes on the back of her head."

Isabella wasn't done dishing out her warnings to the children. "If the two of you cannot get along, I will tie you both together for the day and make you…"

Isabella stopped. Her cheeks turned red as she turned toward me. "Oh, Zura, I am so sorry. That is the last thing that you need to have as a reminder. It was insensitive," Isabella said.

"It's alright," I said into my coffee.

"No, it is not," she continued. "The last thing that you need right now is a reminder about the time that you and Tim were tied together and trying to escape his uncle." Isabella scrambled on with her words quickly. She fervently whipped the eggs in a bowl and poured them into a hot pan.

"Don't be silly. I am quite over the whole thing." I knew that no one in the room believed me, but they were kind enough to let the conversation drop.

After Isabella and I finished cleaning the dishes from breakfast, we left the men with the children to go to visit Momma. We found her in her garden pulling weeds and singing to herself. Her soft melody was sweet to my ears. I had forgotten how beautifully she sings.

Momma's wheat-colored hair, that is starting to turn silver, falls in tendrils around her small face. Time has added very few lines around her eyes and lips. She calls them laugh lines from a lifetime of happiness.

Momma shaded her eyes from the sun and squinted up at us. "Well, to what do I owe the pleasure of my two daughters' company today?" Momma avoided eye contact with me.

"Momma. Can we talk?" I asked.

"Alright, Zura, what should we talk about?" I knew that Momma was angry and hurt by the way that I handled things yesterday. I didn't blame her.

Isabella sensed the tension between Momma and me. "Why don't the three of us go into the house and have a lovely cup of tea," Isabella said.

"Momma stood and wiped her hands on her apron. "Alright. I'll boil some water for tea."

Momma led the way up the porch steps and into the kitchen.

We sat around the kitchen table. I traced a dent in the table's wood that has been there as far back as I can remember.

Isabella efficiently tried to get us through the worst of the conversation. "Zura, why don't you start us off? Is there something that you would like to say?"

I cleared my throat and made eye contact with my mother. "Momma, I am truly sorry for the things that I said to you yesterday. I let all my feelings of ineffectiveness in my children's life interfere in my relationship with you. The past is the past, and I should have kept it that way. I am truly sorry that I upset you. I love you Momma. I hope that you can forgive me."

Momma lay her hand over mine and then rubbed my cheek. "My dear Zura, I am sorry for not being a better mother to you. A lot of what you said was true. I was an absent mother. I did give you way too much freedom, and I cared more about the elephants than I should. I still do. You were always independent and defiant. Like the time that you brought Cha-cha home with you. You were there in the jungle near a jaguar. You brought an injured wild dog with you. Even after your father told you that you could not keep it, you ignored him and stood your ground. Does that remind you of anyone else that you know?"

"Olivia."

"Yes, she was raised on the story of your childhood. It's still her favorite story. Though she tells me that I never tell it as good as you. You must know that she is getting older and she knows that it is not just a random story. She knows that it is your life. Imitation is the best compliment. Someday you will be grateful to have a strong child. It will do her good in life."

"I know that you are right, Momma. Still, I feel like I never handle the situations in the best way."

Momma looked over at Isabella and back to me. "Take Izzy for instance. She's a good mother to Little Peter, Cora, and Kara." Momma smiled from ear to ear. "She will be a great mother to her next child," Momma giggled.

Isabella brought her hand to her belly. "How did you know? I wanted to surprise you!"

"Oh, you don't get to be my age without noticing the signs of blooming motherhood."

"Am I that obvious?"

Momma and I answered at the same time. "Yes," we both said with a laugh.

CHAPTER 2

There is nothing like the feminine sisterhood. The stories, the laughter, the bonding that happens when women share the impending birth of a new child.

Momma is always quick to point out that my birth was a simple affair without unnecessary fussing. "Zura's birth almost happened right in the field. I was charting when my water broke. Thank goodness Peter stayed very close to me in the last few weeks of the pregnancy."

"He was out in the field with you?" I questioned the first time she told this story.

"Well, yes. He has always been attentive and responsible."

This time, as she recounted my birth yet again, I saw a shimmer in Momma's eyes that caused me to ask. "Is Father feeling alright? I get the feeling that he is not sharing something."

"Your father is fine. We are just getting older, Zura. Nothing for you to worry about."

"Are you sure? He didn't look fine yesterday."

"He was just scared for us. That's all. Nothing is going to happen to Peter. Now, I want to share a story for you, Isabella, about Olivia's birth," Momma interrupted with a smile.

Because she has assisted with both of the births of my children and all three of Isabella's she is the keeper of the memories.

Her tactics for avoidance work for now, and I dropped the subject of my father.

Momma likes to tell the story of Olivia's birth, where I was so scared and inexperienced.

"Olivia was anxious to enter this world and came two weeks early. She was not waiting for anything to pass her by; just like her mother." Momma lay her hand on mine.

I had to nod and smile in agreement. "I barely had time to mentally prepare before she was making her grand entrance into the world. Seeing births in nature and going through it yourself are completely different. But my life has been a blessing ever since that day. It's funny, but even before Olivia was born, she tested me and has never stopped for one minute. Between the monkey, sneaking out of the house at night, and fighting with Charlie, I feel like all I ever do is scold her."

Momma shifts in her chair. "Her tenacity. I love that about her soul. Olivia is always testing the waters, wanting to push things just a little farther. She has inherited your quest for exploration."

"True."

"So, you just have to keep setting boundaries and hold her to your rules," Momma said.

Isabella began to giggle in her tea. "She is every bit of your spirit," Isabella chimed in.

"Yeah, well, I did spend almost the entire time with morning sickness and swollen feet with Olivia. I only hope to be a good mother to both of my children. It's something that I worry about; not being good enough."

Momma refilled our tea. "Now, Charlie was a slow and easy pregnancy. You barely complained the entire time."

"Maybe because I knew what to expect. Charlie was easy. He is growing so quickly."

"Yes, he sure is and learning to stand up to his sister," Isabella said.

"But Charlie is exactly like Matt. Both are laid back, happy and content to sit lazily and listen to others, to be in the background, and to take long uninterrupted naps. Jungle life moves at a much slower pace for them."

Momma turned her attention toward Isabella. "How is Tim handling the pregnancy? We already know how you will handle it. You are amazingly organized and prepared."

Isabella sat rubbing her stomach. "Well, that may not be true this time. Having three children already is making me nervous about adding one more into our structured family."

Momma and I shared a look and both laughed. Momma sat forward and took a sip of her cooling tea. "My dear Izzy. You are the master of organization and running a successful household. Just look at the way everyone follows your lead. If anyone can add one or more to her house, it's you."

"Thank you, Momma, that means a lot to me," Isabella said.

After a light lunch with Momma, Isabella and I begin to walk back to my house.

Isabella, a stickler for timeliness and order, wanted to gather her children within the hour and take them home for their lunch and a nap.

As we walked down the path, we gathered Golden Cleome that grows along the trail. It's thin yellow petals, purple center, and protruding stamens make the herb a beautiful addition to my kitchen needs. We eat them as a vegetable and use them for medicines.

We also cut some Krantz Aloe to use for stomach ailments for our families.

Wild ginger grows in abundance and we are particularly interested in gathering it for a host of ailments, and for adding flavoring to our cooking.

Busy in our work, we talked and laughed as we traveled to the edge of my home. As we circled the side of the house, I noticed several strangers standing with Matt and Tim.

Isabella and I stopped to assess the foreigners. Three men and a woman stood at the bottom of my porch steps.

Tim looked relaxed in their company. He gave away nothing, with his hands on his hips and a light laughter.

Matt put Charlie down to play with Tim's brood. I saw one of the men shake hands with Matt and Tim and everyone was smiling.

Immediately, I knew that they were the visitors that wanted to talk about the Tembo Project. They have arrived from America to meet me and my family. I felt a nervous twinge in my stomach as I assessed the strangers.

That's when I took more notice of her. A petite, well-dressed woman positioned herself next to a taller man. Her short, sharp black hair and her flawless, gleaming white skin stood out against the backdrop of wildlife. She had painted red lips and rouged cheeks. Her lashes look long and black, like a spider's legs.

I instantly disliked the way her tiny nose turned up at the end and the way she stared at Matt and touched his arm with a flirty laugh.

Matt's rugged good looks and that dimple when he smiles always warms my heart. I certainly don't like the thought of another woman having that same sensation.

Isabella nudged me. "Would you look at her outfit," she whispered. "Who would wear that much white in a jungle? She obviously has never spent much time out of her home and in the wild."

"Out of her country is more like it," I answered. "I don't like this."

Isabella and I joined arms to become a united front and circled the house to join the strangers and our husbands.

"And there she is!" Matt exclaimed. He walked the short distance to me and put his arm around my waist; probably because he knew that I do not fare well with strangers.

"Here I am," I said unenthusiastically, not taking my gaze off of the woman. The sharpness of her dark brown eyes reminded me of an angry gorilla. Her disingenuous smile was hiding a secret or a deception or a lie.

The taller man stepped forward and extended his hand to me. When our hands joined, the pressure of his handshake was strong and deliberate. "So nice to finally meet you! My name is Alexander Bartell."

"Nice to meet you, Mr. Bartell." I shook his hand with just as much force.

"Call me Alex, please. I think we will be spending a lot of time getting to know one another. I have been waiting for what feels like forever to finally meet the jungle girl responsible for all the buzz in Chicago," he said, showing me his perfect wide-tooth smile. "Why, your story is spoken in every social circle on the south side of the city, and now there is talk of you as far as California. I heard before we left that Hollywood has weighed in, and some important executives see films in the future. Everyone wants to get involved in your plight to save the African Elephants. You're a hit, doll."

Matt squeezed my arm. "We are certainly proud of Zura and her passion for the Tembo Project. She was able to turn grief into a productive plan. Zura's strength and devotion is commendable."

I turned and searched Matt's eyes, finding nothing but adoration for me.

Alex touched my arm and I flinched. "Yes, it does take a special person to turn a tragedy into a life-long plan for revenge," he stated.

I took a step backward, feeling suddenly caged in. His use of words startled and concerned me. "Revenge? I am not out for revenge against the poachers. I want to create awareness, to ask other caring human beings for their help in ending the unnecessary bloodshed of elephants, as well as other poached animals. As for your Hollywood and Chicago, all my information about these places can fit in one of those newspaper articles that Tim gets shipped in every few months. I have no need or desire for that sort of life for me or my family."

Alex paused and cleared his throat. "Perhaps revenge was too strong of a word, Mrs. Jones. I only meant that you braved the jungle with the poachers, and you survived. You were put through hell, and yet grew up to be a strong woman caring for your family and all these animals. And look at you! Gorgeous bronzed skin, tall, long legs. You are what every woman wants to be. May I call you Zura?"

"I was in far more danger in the hands of those men than the jungle. Why does the length of my legs help save the elephants? That's ridiculous. Yes, you may call me Zura," I countered.

"Because you are the spokesperson that people will relate to. You are exotic and wild, and people will be falling all over themselves to give to your cause. That's the way that the world works, doll. If you want to be noticed, you have to be worth noticing.

I drew an imaginary line between us, just waiting for him to cross it.

The woman stepped forward and extended her right hand to me. Her red painted smile looked as phony as the blood red color of her nails. "My name is Alice. Alice Smith. It is great to meet you, Jane."

"It's Zura." I responded, taking her hand and squeezing harder than my normal handshake. "Zura Jones," I answered harshly, and I tried to swallow my dislike for the woman. Referring to me as Jane did nothing to change my opinion of the prissy woman.

Matt sensed my hardening stature and gently squeezed my shoulders for support. "Well, now that we are acquainted, maybe we can enjoy a refreshment," Matt said.

Olivia skipped down the porch steps and ran to Matt and me with her arms full of her furry friend. Jeena is wrapped in Olivia's favorite blanket. The only part of Jeena that is visible is the end of her tail sticking out next to Olivia's knees.

The woman bent down to Olivia, who stood smiling and staring up at Alice. Olivia's dimples showed as she beamed her prettiest grin, and she swung her curls as she bounced with an abundance of energy. "Hi. I am Olivia and I am six."

"Well, hello, Miss Olivia. It is so nice to meet you," Alice said, patting Olivia's head. "And what do you have there? Is this your baby doll? They have baby dolls in this under-developed country?" Alice looked from Alex to me.

Olivia squealed with delight. "Jeena isn't a baby doll" she said, unwrapping the blanket. "She's my baby monkey!"

Jeena, startled by Olivia's quick movements, flew out of the blanket and scurried up Alice's arm.

Alice jolted backward and screamed as Jeena found a place on Alice's shoulder. "Get it off!" Alice yelled. "Someone help me! Alex, I hate crawling things. Grab this little beast before it bites me and I end up with some sort of strange jungle fever!"

I could not help but look over at Isabella and laugh. "You came to the wrong place if you hate things that crawl. We are infested with them," I told her. "In this under-developed country," I added with sarcasm.

Isabella's giggle was contagious and we both were happy to find fault in the almost-perfect-looking Alice Smith.

Matt grabbed Jeena from Alice's shoulder and handed the monkey to Olivia. "Take Jeena over to Charlie and play with him, Olivia. You go now and play."

"But Daddy! Charlie doesn't know how to treat a baby. He is one too. He might hurt Jeena."

"Olivia. Now," Matt countered and Olivia knew by his tone not to argue with her father. She slipped away without another word.

"Precious child." Alice wiped at her shoulder with her crisp-white handkerchief. "I can see that being raised in the wild has led your children into a more primitive lifestyle."

I was feeling as protective as a mother gorilla, ready to pounce on Alice for her snide comments. "Why, whatever do you mean?" I was going in for the kill. "There are many tribes who live out in that jungle," I said, nodding my head toward the tree line, "who paint their faces and where decorative ornaments around their necks and wrists and on their ears in an attempt to make themselves more desirable to the opposite sex. Not so much unlike what you do with your lip and cheek rouge and jewelry." My eyes bored into hers. I was furious on the inside, but calm and deliberate on the outside, and the plastered grin on my face. It told Matt I was back on form. He gave me a subtle squeeze and I could tell he was holding back a chuckle. "Or when you say 'primitive', do you mean happy and free to grow up and to learn how to endure in the harshest of circumstances? To be able to survive using their wits and journey wherever their heart takes them, then yes, my family is growing up very primitive. They are better for it. Why are you here? I am not clear what your part will be in the Tembo Project, Miss Smith."

Alice straightened up before she spoke. "I am a writer. I will be documenting our time here and your trip to the United States. We will be spending a lot of time together, Zura. We should set some ground rules."

I can no longer hide my dislike of Alice. "How dare you come to my home and talk to me about ground rules. Ground rules? We don't need rules. I will decide who I speak to about my family, about my life. So far, I am not exactly trusting you enough to share anything.

And times in the United States? I have no idea what you are referring to, but I have no intention of leaving my home to travel anywhere. I have never agreed to do more than talk to you. I never agreed to go anywhere!" I looked to Matt and searched his face for answers. Matt's face told a story that he knew they wanted me to travel. I moved a step away from my husband. "I am liking the idea less and less every minute. You knew?"

Alexander let out a chuckle. "Now ladies. We are all hoping that you become fast friends. Let's not start out on the wrong foot."

Matt cleared his throat. "Why don't we all go inside and have some tea. "Zura and Izzy, could we bother you to prepare tea and something to eat for our guests?"

"Certainly," I said without enthusiasm and through my clenched teeth.

Isabella and I turned and went into the house. I let the screened door slam behind me to let Matt know that I was displeased with being dismissed and about his decision to hide aspects of this visit from me.

Isabella put out some food as I prepared the tea. "Can you hear her giggle? She is obnoxious, arrogant and rude."

I have to smile at Isabella's hatred for Alice on my behalf. "I have never seen you this worked up before," I laughed. "You sound as mad as I am, Sister."

"Sisters have to stick together," Isabella smiled.

I fought the urge to add a little something extra in Alice's drink to make her have intestinal troubles. I settled for knowing that she knows nothing about this jungle and its dangers. I took pleasure in knowing she hates things that crawl and her entire trip in Africa will be filled with crawly things.

"Is it safe to enter?" Matt says, peeking his head through the doorway. He wore a goofy smile that made it impossible for me to stay angry for long.

"Zura, I am sorry that all of this was sprung on you like that. It was not my intention to let you hear their ideas like that."

"Matt, I can't leave my home. I just can't."

"You don't have to make up your mind now, sweetheart. Let's just listen to Alex and Alice before you have them eaten by lions."

"By lions," I mutter. "She'd give them a stomach ache for sure."

We gathered around the table with Alex sitting across from me, and Alice to his right. Matt sat on one side of me and Tim on the other. The other men have not been introduced and they stayed outside. Instead of participating, Isabella decided to watch the children so they wouldn't be a distraction, and for that I was thankful.

Alexander cleared his throat. "I am so excited for this opportunity. This has been a life-long dream to come here." He took a sip of the tea and continued. "Mmm, that's very nice. What's it called?"

"Tea," I say cynically before Matt nudged my arm.

Alexander remained oblivious to my sarcasm and continued. "I represent some large investors that are interested in taking the Tembo Project to the next level."

"Why?" I ask.

"Why, what?"

"Why do they want to take this to the next level?"

"Because it is the right thing to do. Those suffering animals need our protection. Because your story has reached a large audience."

"I think there is more truth in the fact that there is money to be made. You can't protect them. Believe me, I know. We can only try," I answered from experience.

Alexander removed his hat and placed it on the table. "If you can't protect them, then why did you start the Tembo Project?"

"In honor of my beloved elephant, Tembo. He was murdered several years ago."

"Yes, I know that. I read the article about you in the paper. Isn't that what the Tembo Project was designed to do?"

"The Tembo Project is to create awareness and hopefully a passion for the elephants that can help to create stiffer laws, more protection for elephants and other animals poached as prizes."

"And that is exactly why you need to go with us to the States. We need you to be the spokesperson for the animals that cannot speak for themselves. We need your energy and look, and everything about you that screams 'Jungle Girl on a Mission.'"

Charlie opened the screened door and came to me. "Mommy, Jeena scratched me."

I rise and scoop Charlie into my arms. "Excuse me everyone, my son needs me," I said and carried Charlie outside with me.

I sat on the steps beside Isabella with Charlie on my lap. "Let me see where Jeena scratched you, Charlie," I said. He showed me several long, thin pink lines on his arm.

"I tried to pick her up and she scratched me," Charlie reported. "She wants to bite me. Olivia said so."

"I will talk with Olivia. How did you try to pick her up?"

"By the tail."

I am beginning to understand the reason Jeena may have scratched Charlie. "Charlie, you never grab a monkey by the tail. That scares her, and it might hurt Jeena, alright?"

Charlie nodded his head. "Can I go play now?"

"Stay where I can see you. Stay with Cora and Kara, okay?"

Charlie nodded again and slid down my extended legs.

"A man of few words," I said to Isabella.

She looked at me quizzically. "What is that all about?"

"Just a scratch."

"Not Charlie. The visitors."

"Oh, they are trying to convince me to go to the United States."

I looked over at the two men standing at a distance and noticed they were staring back at Isabella and me."

"What do you think about those two?" I gestured with my head.

Isabella looked in their direction. "They look intense; maybe a little scary. They remind me of Chicago hitmen. One is all muscles and the other is pretty pudgy, but he looks mean."

I nodded my head in agreement. "Guards or something. We don't even know their names. Isn't that strange if they are traveling with Alex for him not to introduce us to his associates?"

"I think it's very strange."

"Did you see the pistols on their belts? They don't try to hide them."

"No, it's almost like they want everyone to see them. You would think it would make us feel safe with poachers in the area. You know, to have more people to guard us. But that's the last thing I feel when I look at those men. Or maybe they think we primitives need their protection."

Izzy laughed. "Yeah, that's exactly what I was thinking."

Olivia walked a little too close to them for my liking. I see her holding up Jeena for them to see. One of the men bent down to Olivia's level and talked to her. He patted her head before she skipped away.

I shook my head. "My child has no fear."

"Never. Maybe that's good and maybe that's a bad thing."

"With the little we know about those men; I am going to say it's a bad thing. I need to keep a close eye on those two. I don't want them close to our children."

"Me either," Isabella said. "I am going to take Little Peter and the girls home with me, if you don't mind. They need food and the girls need a nap."

"No, of course I don't mind. Thank you for watching all of them for the short conversation I had with Alex and Alice. I will let you know if anything else happens."

Isabella gathered her children and left with a wave. I instinctively called for Olivia and Charlie to join me on the porch. "Let's have a story time."

"Yes!" Olivia excitedly sat beside me on the porch steps.

"What story should we tell?"

"Tell me about Jane," Olivia answered.

I waited on the porch until Alex and Alice left my home. Alice avoided eye contact with me and muttered a farewell. Alex took my hand and brought it to his lips for a kiss. "Until I see you again," he whispered, and turned to leave.

I was too exhausted to discuss the day's events with Matt. After taking his shift guarding the field from the poachers, we went about the rest of the day as if the conversation about leaving Africa never happened.

After the sunset, I got my children ready for bed. Charlie is easy. I cleaned him and put him into his night clothing. He required a hug and a kiss, and he fell asleep easily.

Olivia is another story. She wants to avoid sleep at all cost. I am hoping that now that she can keep Jeena with her, that she will fall asleep and stay asleep.

"Tell me a story," Olivia tucked Jeena in tightly against her and smiled up at me. I brushed her curls from her eyes. "What story would you like to hear?"

"Tell me the story about Jane!" Olivia sunk a little lower into her bed.

I was not in the mood for the Jane story again. "I already told you that story this afternoon. I will tell you about the silly monkeys."

"Alright. Jeena will like that one." She adjusted the blanket from Jeena's ears to ensure that she heard the story. I rubbed Olivia's feet to help her to relax.

"There once was a troop of silly monkeys that lived in the jungle's trees.
They played and swung from the branches of the Jackalberrys.
Kiume led the troop of monkeys and he was full of pride.
He taught the littlest monkeys to run from danger and hide.
Kiume showed them how to climb so high and hide in the big leaves.
To keep their voices quiet, until his order they received.

When all was safe, and the danger left, the troop could then play on.
But silence and stillness were what they learned until the threat was gone.

One little monkey named Jabari was clever as clever could be.
He never liked to listen to Kiume or his loving mommy.
Jabari was brave but clumsy when he raced his brothers quite fast.
Never afraid to reach too far, he didn't want to come in last.

One day, Kiume called out to say that danger was very near.
The monkeys raced to the treetops to hide in the leaves in fear.
But Jabari was always fearless, and he climbed down the tree instead.
He wanted to see the leopard and bounce upon its head.

He climbed a little closer until the leopard was in sight.
And when the leopard saw Jabari, he took a little bite.
Jabari's tail was bitten clean off. In the leopard's mouth it lay.
Jabari raced into the treetops, but he barely got away.

*The leopard stopped chasing Jabari, because the limbs were
way too thin.
He climbed back down to eat his meal before Jabari inter-
rupted him.
Jabari had learned his lesson, he kept to the tops of the trees.
Never interrupt a leopard who eats whatever he sees.*

*His pride was replaced with wisdom, to know what he had to do.
It's a very good lesson for monkeys, and also for me and for you."*
Olivia's eyes were heavy with sleep. "What's wisdom, Mommy?"
"Wisdom is knowing what to do and listening to your parents."
"Do I have wisdom?" Olivia yawned.
"Yes. Every time you do what we tell you, you have wisdom."
"Someday I want to be like Jabari and climb the trees to the top."
"I do not want you to be like Jabari, Olivia."
"But why Mommy? Don't you think I can climb?"
"You are my daughter, of course you can climb." I brushed her
silky curls from her face for a second time.
"Then why, Mommy?"
I tickled her belly. "Because I don't want you to lose your tail!"
Olivia giggled a sweet little laugh that showed those dimples on
her cheeks.
I kissed her on her head. "Good night, my little monkey."
"Good night, Mommy." Olivia cuddled Jeena close and closed
her eyes.

There was a buzz of activity so early in the morning. Charlie and
Olivia were fed, dressed and playing nicely together. Matt was taking
his turn watching for the poachers in the field, and I was preparing
food for the evening meal.

Matt had invited the visitors to eat with us without talking to me
first. He knew what my answer would have been; I had no intention
of entertaining these strangers, but I am doing the right thing and
preparing extra food for them to make Matt happy.

I had stepped out onto the porch for a breath of fresh air when I
spotted Alex coming through the trees. He was waving his hat high
above his head and shouting a hello in my direction.

Alexander Bartell seemed unafraid of the jungle and its inhabitants. It was the way he casually strode through the tall grasses, not looking down at what might be lurking in the bush. He is either very brave or very stupid. My mind was not yet made up on which answer fit.

"Good morning, Zura." Alex called.

"Good morning, Mr. Bartell," I answered.

He had an air about him and a glare in his eyes that darted in all directions, looking for an unknown target. "Alex, please," he smiled but did not make eye contact with me.

Watching people is no different than watching animals. Each has a mannerism distinct to their species. A lion will always act as a lion and attack the gazelle. The gazelle will always run in fear. It instinctively knows that the lion's presence means danger. It is in the look of the eyes.

The lion's eyes are keen, straight forward and deliberate. The gazelle looks from the side of its head, always watching for dangerous situations. Their eyes are always wide and wary.

For some reason, I felt like a gazelle around Alex. I was unsure of when he would pounce like a lion. I felt as though he looked at me as prey.

Human beings will always act as humans. Sometimes laughing, enjoying their time with each other. They give off a positive vitality, while others give off an equal amount of a powerful energy of anger, dislike, or hatred.

Alex's face looked happy, with a smile of straight, white teeth. But his eyes tell a different story. They are dark and dangerous. Those traits cannot be hidden from anyone who looks for them. I have seen eyes like that before…

Alex reached the bottom of the porch steps and stood with his hands on his hips. "What a wonderful start to the day." He breathed deep and exhaled with exaggeration. "Walking in the jungle, hearing the calls of the birds; the monkeys. They certainly are a loud bunch. I think one of the monkeys urinated on one of my men's heads this morning. Very amusing. Why, it is no wonder that you like it here, doll. It is splendid. Splendid indeed."

"I am partial to it, yes."

"Why, I bet you know every inch of this jungle. Every path. Every secret spot. The call of every animal."

"I have my favorite places. I know the animals well, yes. This jungle is too large for me to know every inch of it, but I can find my way." I was again guarding my answers, unable to determine whether he is making small talk or if he has a purpose to his observations which he would later use to my disadvantage without my knowledge. I didn't want him to 'quote' me.

Alex leaned forward to place his arm on the step railing. "Are they the cave and the cliffs that are mentioned in the article about you? What do you call it? Thinking Rock, I believe it is? What does it feel like to stand at the top of that cliff and look over its side?"

I am not sure why Alexander is so interested in my past. There is no enjoyment for me in the conversation. "Is there something that brought you here so early this morning, Alex?"

"You."

"Excuse me?"

"I guess I was hoping and excited that perhaps we could talk about the trip to the United States. Alice has some suitable clothing that I am sure she wouldn't mind letting you borrow. There, of course, will be dinners and meetings, interviews and special appearances. We can get you all dolled up when we get to the states. We can cut that hair, apply some rouge to your cheeks and dress you up quite nicely. You have an amazing figure, so dressing you will not be an issue. Not to worry. Everything will be handled." Alexander reached out and rubbed my arm.

It felt sharp and intrusive. I stepped backward in response to his unwanted touch. "Alex, I have not given my answer, but you should know that I am unable to leave my family. My children need me. It is just not possible when they are so small. They need their mother, and I need them."

"Yes, your children are quite a handful, by the looks of them. It is a shame that your husband or your family is not capable of tending to your children for a short time for you to follow your dreams."

"Don't you mean your dreams? You know nothing of my dreams. My place is here. My husband is an excellent father and is very well equipped to tend to our children's needs at any time in any place. Don't mistake his kindness for something else."

"Oh, yes, of course he is. Tell me, where is Matt? I want to have a chat with him before he gets caught up in his work."

"Matt went to the field. There were some poachers here the other night and he is making sure that they are no longer in the area."

I felt my temper rising to the surface, like a pot of boiling water hissing and bubbling. Alex is dismissing the conversation and giving my opinion on the matter no more important than an idle thought. "Alice can keep her clothing." Again, the plastic smile appeared on my face to match his own. "She's not my style. And going to the United States is not my dream. Why would I leave this primitive paradise?" I spread my arms to take in the jungle. Then the smile disappeared and I was all business. "Make no mistake, Alexander." I drew his full name out slowly to stress it. "My husband and I discuss things of importance, but I'll make the final decision in this matter. Go to him if you like, but don't think you'll be able to convince him to persuade me one way or the other. We don't work that way."

"Of course, of course. But it is everyone's dream to seek new and adventurous places. You would have to be insane to want to spend the rest of your life never experiencing the finer things."

"Mr. Bartell, life doesn't get more adventurous than the jungle."

Alex reached in his pocket and pulled out a small silver case. Inside, he had cigarettes neatly lined up. He selected one and lit it. He took a long drag and exhaled the foul smoke. "Do you suppose that is why the men from your past came to Africa? Did they come for the thrill of it all?"

"They came for the money, for the thrill of killing, and to do evil, especially Bain. He never cared about anything other than getting rich. They were nasty poachers that got exactly what they deserved. The fact that we are dealing with men shooting near the herd again makes me angry and very sensitive." I spoke as though in warning.

For the first time since he arrived, Alex was silent. He took another long drag on his cigarette and created a circle with the smoke. I watched it whirl skyward until it dissipated.

Alex took a step backward from the porch. "Poachers, you say? Here and now? Real life poachers come to slay a mighty beast? Did they get one? What an excellent addition that would make to the story."

"Mr. Bartell, I would kindly ask you to not speak to me about the slaying of any animal. Their unnecessary killing to become a trophy on a wall, like Tim's uncle had in their home, is despicable."

Alex chuckled. "There she is. There is that Jungle Girl that everyone is talking about. That's why we need you. You have the spirit of a warrior. Yes, it must be you. I won't take no for an answer," Alex said walking in the direction of the field. "Good day to you, Jungle Girl!" he called with a tip of his hat.

CHAPTER 3

The children and I were entering the barn where we house the new elephants, when one of my favorite elephants and Tembo's brother, Kendi, appeared from behind the barn. His lumbering gate excited Olivia and she started to hop around with the monkey on her shoulder. "Kendi!" she yelled. "I want to say hello to Kendi, Mommy! He likes it when I rub his trunk."

"Go ahead. But be careful, Olivia. Remember what Mommy told you about approaching the elephants."

"Take it slow and whisper." She lowered her voice and tiptoed toward Kendi.

"Correct. And why do we whisper?" I matched the softness of her voice with my own.

"So that we don't scare them, and they won't jump in the air and land on our heads."

I laughed at Olivia's reasoning. "That's right. We don't want elephants on our heads."

I propped open the barn door and stepped inside. The smell of fresh grasses filled my senses. But there was something else in the air—metallic and familiar.

I opened the pen to a stall and the little elephant walked out of the pen. She made her way out of the door. Olivia squealed with delight and yelled Maji's name. *So much for whispering*, I thought.

Starting on my chores, I began to muck Maji's pen. I was replacing the grasses in the pen, when Charlie waddled over to me.

Charlie placed a hand on my leg, and I noticed it left my leg feeling sticky. I wiped at it with my hand and the reddish color caught my attention. Blood! Blood covered my hand, and smeared on my leg.

I nervously peered down at Charlie. He had blood on his hands, his face, in his hair, and all over the front of his shirt. "Charlie!" I yelled It startled him and he began to cry.

I was petrified. What caused all this blood? I quickly removed his shirt and found no evidence of a cut or any kind of injury. I grabbed his crimson hands and wiped them on my shorts. After examining his little blood-stained hands, I also found no damage. His head and face were clear of harm. I stared at him for a moment and my gaze went to the bloody footprints made by Charlie. I reluctantly followed them to the back of the barn, anxious about what I would find.

As I see the reason for the large amount of blood, I covered Charlie's eyes to the horror, though I am thoroughly aware that he has already seen the carnage. One of the orphaned elephants that arrived only a week ago is lying dead in its own pool of blood. Its throat is sliced open and its opened eyes have dulled.

"Ssh. Baby sleeping," Charlie said and put a blood-stained finger to his lips. I grabbed Charlie's hand and removed it away from his face.

"Let's go get you cleaned up," I said and turned from the scene.

I raced toward the door. Olivia is outside placing Jeena on top of Maji and directing Maji to walk in circles. "Look Mommy. I am training Maji!"

"Good job, Olivia. Stay right there and play with Maji."

Olivia looked up and appeared horrified when she saw a blood-covered Charlie.

Charlie was crying and Olivia was now screaming.

"Mommy! Charlie was poached! Those bad men poached my brother!" Olivia began to wail.

"No. Your brother is alright, Olivia. It is not his blood. Charlie is not hurt. I am just going to clean him off."

I took Charlie to a large bucket that we use to collect rainwater. Filling a smaller bucket, I stripped off Charlie's clothes and dunked him into the refreshing water. His crying turns to wailing as I tried to remove the blood as quickly as possible.

Olivia ran over to stare in at the water. "The water is pink, Mommy. Why is it pink?"

"It is pink because it has blood in it. Pink water is never good water. Only clean fresh water is good water. Do you understand?"

"But if Charlie didn't get poached, where did all the blood come from?" Olivia asked.

"Pink water is bad, Mommy," Charlie repeated.

I cannot answer Olivia. The scene is too fresh. The vision of that poor baby elephant came flooding back. This was no ordinary poaching. Baby elephants do not have tusks, nor did they take anything as a trophy. They had entered the barn intentionally.

Olivia looked from Charlie to the water and back to me. Her expression changed as her mind figured it out. "No!" She yelled and took off running toward the barn.

"Olivia, stop!" I called out to her as I picked Charlie up from the water and ran toward the barn. "Olivia, come back here! Stay out of the barn!"

She didn't listen to my plea and ran right into the barn. I immediately heard her let out a feral howl. She had seen the dead elephant lying on its side. "Mommy, the baby is bleeding! Help her, Mommy!" She had thrown herself on top of the baby elephant, wailing. The scene reminded me of the day I found Tembo poached in the field. That had crushed my heart. Now my children have both witnessed this horror.

Olivia's smooth little hand rubbed the wrinkled skin of the elephant and she cried. She was kneeling in the blood; her blond curls soaked up the stickiness. She raised her head to look at me.

I felt the bile rising in my throat from the murderous scene. Although my children are uninjured. I can no longer stomach the sight of them covered in blood.

"Mommy, the baby hurt her neck. Help her," Olivia sobbed and placed her hands on the wound as if to apply pressure. Jeena ran through the blood and scurried up to Olivia's shoulder. She began to lick her paws to remove the sticky mess from her fur. That's when the first wave of nausea consumed me. I turned my head and vomited on the ground of the barn. My hands were still full with Charlie and I'm pretty sure my boots or maybe even my leg was splashed with vomit.

I adjusted a naked Charlie to sit on my hip as pink water ran down my leg. I grabbed Olivia with my free hand. Her hand was slick with blood and slid easily out of my grasp. "Olivia, we have to go and get this off of us. The smell of blood may attract lions or hyenas. Come with me, baby. It is going to be alright. Mommy will make it better. We have to go find Daddy or Uncle Tim."

"You can't make it better!" she yelled as I successfully pulled her away from the elephant. "You should have helped her!"

I was too stunned by Olivia's hurt and anger to respond. Somehow in her mind I was to blame for the death of the baby elephant. I couldn't help remembering I blamed my own mother for the loss of Tembo, didn't I?

I made it outside with vomit on my leg and my two blood-covered children who were still crying. When I looked up, I saw Matt and Alex looking at me and my children in horror.

Matt ran to us, panic-stricken and shaking. "Zura! What has happened?" Matt's eyes searched our surroundings before they landed again on my own. "All this blood! Were you attacked by something? Where are you hurt? Tell me, Zura," he said grabbing both sides of my face. "Who or what has done this to you?"

Olivia slipped from my hands and latched herself to Matt's leg. "Daddy! The new elephant is poached! Daddy, help her!"

Matt searched my face for the truth. I can only nod and try to calm Charlie by swaying my body and holding him close.

What a scene we must have been for Alex. My family, standing outside of the barn with blood on all of us. The word primitive came to mind as I passed Charlie to Matt to try to compose myself.

Alex stood with his hand raised to his mouth. I feared that if he became sick, I would also start vomiting.

Alex looked as if he was witnessing a murder himself. "Who would do this? How did this happen?"

I ignored his questions and searched Matt's face for an answer. He picked up Olivia with his spare arm. "Let's get them in the house and clean off this blood. We will figure this out."

I nodded and grabbed Charlie from Matt.

I began to walk toward the house with my son in my arms, Alex following close behind.

He cleared his throat. "If I may," he began

I turned quickly and sharply to address Alex. "You may not! Don't. Just don't say a word! Not now!"

After we were all freshly washed, we put the children down for a nap and they did not protest.

I stood on my porch, my hair still wet and pulled back from my face in a braid. My skin tingles from being scrubbed to a pink hue. No matter how hard I scrubbed, the scene replayed itself inside of my head.

Matt was talking with Alex and Tim. Their words were inaudible, but Matt's hand was pointing at the barn, then he made a gesture that looked like he was explaining how he found me with Charlie in my arms and Olivia by my side.

I looked away to see Father frantically running toward my house, my mother followed closely behind him. Momma quickly climbed the porch steps and gathered me in for a hug. I cried on her shoulder to release the empty feeling in my heart. I realized that we were swaying. The same motherly sway that I did for my children. "I love you, Momma."

"Ssh, it is going to be alright, Zura." I felt her body's movement as she cried with me over the loss of the elephant.

I looked up to see my father's worried eyes.

"Father, I am alright. No one is hurt. We are just shaken. The children will eventually forget as they age. Charlie will anyway. Olivia is strong. She will be able to learn from this and move past it."

"Who would do this?"

"I think I know." I said, gazing in Alex's direction.

"You know who?" Momma questioned.

"Well, not exactly who they are. But I suspect that whoever shot at us in the field are the same people that did this heinous act."

"The poachers?" Father shook his head.

Matt stepped forward. "Zura suspects that the poachers from the other day were not actually poachers."

Father looked from Matt to me. "What are you basing this on?"

"As I explained to Matt, anyone trying to poach an animal would have made a better shot. If that was their intent. They completely missed giant, easier targets but were somehow able to almost put a bullet in my head. I think that I was the intended target. I think that they were trying to kill me."

Momma gasped. "Oh, you can't think that. Who would want to hurt you?"

"I don't know the answer to that question. All I know is that they missed the elephants and we had one bullet hit the canteen that was hanging off the bag, one landed by my head before we moved, and one ripped the bark from the tree, followed by more shots in our direction. No hunter would be that bad of a shot. And they wouldn't have fired so many times in such rapid succession. Tim, you know I am right."

Tim nods. "I knew that you were piecing something together. You were doubtful from the beginning, right?"

"I wanted to be wrong. But I am not wrong. Someone cut the throat of that elephant. They knew I would find her, I bet. Or they knew that it would affect me."

"What are you saying?" my father asked.

"I don't know. Maybe someone doesn't like the publicity that I am bringing to the cause. Maybe they are upset about the Tembo Project? Whatever it is, now it has affected my children. That means that it is personal."

"What are you thinking we should do?"

"Put a stop to them before they hurt any of us," I said.

Tim shook his head. "How are we going to do that?"

"We go after them. I can track them, you know I can. I don't think I can still climb the trees and swing through them like I did when I was young, but I can certainly find them. They will be leaving a trail.

Alex approached the porch. "Why don't you leave it to my men to find them. My men can do it, and we can decide what to do with them when they get back."

I made eye contact with Alex. "You said it yourself this morning. I know this jungle, every secret place. I can find them much quicker before they hurt anyone or anything else. Do your men know what to do when a snake bites or how to avoid the predators that will know your every move even before you do? Can they track? "

"Why don't you focus on what you need to do to get ready for our trip and just leave this little incident to the men?" Alex stated.

I felt my eyes sharpen. "Little incident? LITTLE incident?" I was livid. "Why do you think your men are the ones to solve this? I am more capable of tracking them than all of you put together. And the fact that you're so interested in finding these poachers, the fact that you think your men can find them, makes me wonder if you know more than you're telling us."

I looked to Matt for support. He gave me a worried stare. "I can't lose you, Zura. And the children need their mother. Let's take Alex up on his offer and let his men bring the poachers to us."

"That's not how you deal with poachers and you know it as well as I do. You don't bring them to you. You eliminate them." I found myself looking into Tim's knowing eyes.

"Not this time, Sister. There will be no killing this time. We have to do it this way, alright?"

I stormed back into the house. It seemed as if no one understood the seriousness of our situation. I went to check on my children to find them both still napping. Charlie was sucking on his thumb and Olivia was cradling her monkey. They looked peaceful, as if the day's events never happened. I only hoped that when they woke, I could be the mother that they need to help them deal with the tragedy.

Matt sneaked into the room and wrapped his arms around me. He whispered in my ear. "Alex is sending his men now. They know to join him at the airfield to get to the ship for the voyage to the United States. He hopes that you leave with him tomorrow."

He led me to our room for the impending conversation. "This is a perfect time for you to get away. If you truly think that someone is after you, then you should go on the trip to give us time to deal with this. I have every confidence that Alex's men will find whoever did this and we will bring them to justice," Matt smiled.

"You really believe that?"

"Yes, I do. His men are hired security that will be able to track them."

"Fine, then it's settled."

"Wonderful. You will have the time of your life. Just you wait and see." Matt hugged me.

"Oh, you misunderstand."

"Misunderstand what?" He gave me a peculiar look.

"I am not going. You are." I nodded and poked him in the chest.

"You are out of your mind! I can't go."

"Why not? You said it yourself. You have every confidence in his men."

"I do, Zura. But I have to be here with the family."

"More than I do?"

"Well, no. But I have already seen the States. I spent most of my life there."

"Which is exactly why it has to be you. You know the culture, the people and Chicago. I don't. I have no desire to see it. You know my story almost as well as Tim."

"I suppose you want him to go as well?" Matt crossed his hands over his chest.

"That's actually not a bad idea," I said, tapping my lips with my finger.

"Just stop, alright? We cannot desert our families at a time like this. Why, people would think we're cowards, running off to the United States when our women are in danger."

"So, you do still think we are in danger?"

"I already told you that the men will handle it. Do not twist my words." Matt was becoming frustrated. His face was reddening from the conversation that he was losing. Men cannot out-talk or out-think their women.

I walked away and went down to the porch where Tim, Momma and my father were still standing.

Father smiled as if a weight had been taken off his shoulders. "Did Matt tell you that Mr. Bartell's men will be hunting down the poachers and will see that they come to justice?"

"Yes, Matt told me."

Matt made his way to join us on the porch in time to hear my announcement.

"I have decided not to go to the United States. My place is here. Matt will be going instead. I would like Tim to go with him."

Father was furious over my news. "Are you crazy? The men can't leave here right now. We have to make sure that nothing goes wrong."

"Matt has assured me that Alex's men will handle this and meet him at the airfield. There is no reason to worry any longer."

"He is right. They will deal with it." Father said with confidence.

Momma spoke up. "Peter, maybe you should go as well."

They stared at each other. A nonverbal message passed between them.

"Momma, why should Father go?"

"I don't want him to go, of course. But the visit will do him good. It's only for a short time." A tear slid down her cheek.

"Rosie," Father said. "I can't leave you." Father rubbed Momma's cheek.

"You must," Momma whispered.

My suspicions were correct. There is something going on with my father.

"Father, Momma is right. Maybe you should go as well."

Father looked from Momma to me. "You want me to go too?"

"Why not? The women in this family are more than capable of handling things for a few weeks, right Momma?"

Momma was silent. I know that she did not like Father leaving her for so long.

"Momma can stay with me and the kids."

Tim shook his head. "What about Izzy? She is pregnant. I can't leave her now."

"Izzy is more than capable of handling things. We could all go, and she would take care of the houses, children, and animals without giving it a second thought. She is newly pregnant, and you will be back way before the baby is due."

I made a strong argument that left my entire family speechless. I secretly had no confidence in Alex's men and I planned to find the poachers on my own. With the men gone and Momma watching the children, I knew I could travel through the jungle easily until I found them. It has been so long since I've tried to climb trees and swing from branch to branch. I wondered whether I'd lost the ability to move in the trees as I did in my youth. I knew there was only one way that I could answer these questions. I had to test myself before I was put to the test and came up lacking.

I walked into the house and grabbed a cloth bag that I kept for emergency situations. It contained water, bandages, matches, rags, dried leaves to help make a fire, and I placed fruit into it for food.

I grabbed my gun and slid it into the back of my shorts before I rejoined the family. My knife was strapped to my waist and I was ready to go.

I hugged Momma, Father and Matt. "I am going for a walk. I want to be alone with my thoughts. Be back soon," I said, leaving my family there to discuss my idea.

Matt began to protest.

"Zura, we are not done discussing this. Zura!" he yelled.

I raised my hand in the air and continued to walk into the jungle without a backward glance.

I had to focus if I intended to track men in the jungle after Matt, Tim and Father leave.

I had just been in the jungle with Momma when we escaped the shooting, and I did not venture into that part again. The place I was going was much deeper into the jungle. It still held its magic and wonder. *This is my past, my playground, and my pain. It is sacred to me.*

The paths of childhood were almost invisible now. Time has allowed the undergrowth to suffocate the landscape with its vines wrapping their way around everything.

I became completely engulfed in my senses with the sights and smells around me. The dense trees were taller than I remembered. Tall and sturdy, they moved with the breeze that cooled my sweaty skin.

A small stream was too enticing for me to ignore and I lost myself in the coolness of the jungle's water. Spending only a few moments dipping my feet in to cool off, I did not spend an inordinate amount of time exposing my feet to whatever lay within the water. I dried my feet with some rags that I had thrown in my bag. After examining my feet, I carefully examined my legs for anything that may have attached itself to me. I peeled a leech from the back of my calf and threw it into the water. Like everything in nature, leeches have their purpose and can be used to aid in injuries. But I have never been fond of them.

I sat for a moment taking in my surroundings, refreshing my senses to the interior of the jungle floor, its canopy and the myriad sounds. I noticed a path has been cleared by an elephant. Broken branches lay embedded in the jungle floor. I spotted an elephant footprint and smiled. When I was a child, I would take off my shoes and make my footprint in the middle of the elephant's print. Monkeys in the trees jumped and sent a shower odd leaves to float toward me. I noticed the tree in front of me was a perfect climbing tree. The low branches looked strong enough to hold my weight.

I placed my shoes in the bag and threw the pack over my shoulder. Beginning slowly, and climbing carefully to watch my every move, I reached and pulled myself up and over the branch. My hands and feet were cautiously working in unison. Branch by branch, I planned each next step.

I was as high now as I dared to go; the view between the trees is a blanket of leaves, hiding the paths, hiding the animals, the threats, the beauty. And it all came back to me. The feel of the bark under my hands and feet. The smell of the jungle. Birds singing familiar songs; the music took me back and I smiled.

I saw the opportunity to glide to another promising tree, but my reach fell short and I tumbled toward the ground. Luckily, I hit a smaller limb that caught me. Before it broke under my weight, I grabbed another limb and shimmied down the tree. I was not wounded except for my pride. It was saddening to know that I have lost the ability to glide as I did when I was younger.

I put my shoes back on before retracing my steps and sticking to the almost hidden path. I made my way back to familiar terrain.

I walked to the base of the waterfall and Thinking Rock. As a child, I climbed Thinking Rock almost daily, looking for the best ways to reach the top. I recognized its surface as easily as I know my own face.

The powerful waterfall soothed my soul. Its deep base and dangerous depths had always been a refuge for me and is one even now.

The rushing sound of the water spilling over the top is commanding as it drums in my ears.

It hides a secret cave that I cannot wait to see again. Although, after the article in the newspaper, Thinking Rock and the cave were no longer a secret. It was out there for the world to know where I hid Tim from danger and where Bain almost killed me.

I hiked the side of the waterfall, carefully climbing the slick ledges before I entered the cave. I was surrounded by strong deep gray rocks. Its gravelly floor mixed with a sandy material felt good on my heated feet. The coolness of the cave and the refreshing mist from the waterfall at the entrance are wondrous to my heated skin. The only light I can see shines through the prevailing water.

As my eyes adjusted, I saw the wood and dry twigs that I had stacked in the corner when I was a child. I was amazed to find that my emergency fire supplies were still intact. I saw a cloth and I reached down and found my handmade doll. "There you are," I wiped the dusty grime from her sewn face, "I always wondered where I lost you."

I placed her back on the wood pile and fixed her dress around her.

As I turned back to the waterfall, something glimmered from the cave floor. It was the knife that I'd hidden near the cave's entrance. Light reflected off its blade. It is a good buck knife from the United States.

My father thought he had lost it. But I had taken it with me for protection one day and it never left the cave.

I picked it up and wiped the dust from it. The wooden handle was glossy and smooth and fit perfectly in my hand. I ran the tip of my finger over the sharp blade, then placed it on the emergency wood pile with the doll. *Someday it would be nice to bring Olivia here and share this special place with her. I know that she would enjoy discovering this cave and finding the doll.* I smiled when I turned to leave.

CHAPTER 4

The evening came quickly. Decisions needed to be made and I knew I was in for another night of family conversations. The thought on everyone's mind was still who will stay and who will go.

Isabella was in the living room making another fun sleepover for the children. She draped sheets to make tents and gave them some time to play before calling lights out.

Isabella joined the family circle with apprehension on her face. "Did I miss anything?"

"No, we waited for you," I said.

Momma cleared her throat. "I don't understand why we are discussing this."

Father patted her hand. "Because this is important. Getting support to stop the bloodshed of these animals has been our mission since we came here, Rosie. It has been our life task to care for them, study them and take in their young. I believe there is no question that as a family, we have to follow our calling and do everything we can to help them."

"Then Zura and Matt should go. We can keep the kids," Momma stated, changing her mind about Father's departure. It was predictable that Momma couldn't be without Father for so long.

"You just don't want Father to go," I raised my voice.

Momma lowered her gaze. "No, I do not. It's shameful. But you don't understand it all."

"I am not leaving my children, Momma. I cannot. You know it's true. Especially with what happened in the barn. They must be traumatized. I am not leaving them now. Matt, Tim, I would at least like you to go. You can easily sell our story to anyone willing to listen. You both are charming and great businessmen. Use those brains that brought the two of you together in college and find a way to grow the Tembo Project. Do it for me. Do it for all of us."

Matt nodded his head. "Alright, darling. We will do this for you."

Tim looked at Isabella and she nodded.

"Alright. I will go. Tim said. "Zura, you must make sure that Izzy doesn't overdo it. She tends to think she can handle anything."

I smiled at her before turning to Tim. "She can."

Father stood and began to pace as he usually does when things are stressful. "I will also go with you. I believe that you could use my experiences in the field as a reference to the killing and the orphans left behind."

Father looked from me to Momma. "My Rosie, you will have your daughters and grandchildren to keep you busy. I have to go, you know I do. We will only be gone for a few weeks."

Momma apprehensively nodded her head but remained silent.

The next morning was filled with packing and sadness. Our men were ready to leave when Alex arrived. "Change your mind, Jungle Girl?" Alex was hopeful.

"No, my place is here."

"It's a shame. You could be big in the States."

"I can be big right here," I said and turned from him.

One of Father's helpers prepared to drive them to the airfield.

We said our goodbyes with kisses and long hugs.

Olivia stood watching the truck start to drive away. "Good bye, Daddy! Please bring me a baby doll when you come home!" she yelled.

"I will! Take care of Charlie and no fighting."

It was as if someone let the wind out of Olivia's sails. "I will try."

Matt laughed. "Try hard."

He blew me a kiss and they drove away.

My emotions were split. Part of me was relieved that I did not have to make that trip and another part was sad to be without my beloved Matt's company for a few weeks, or even one day. But I knew I would throw myself into spending time with Momma and the children.

I also knew that telling Momma that I would be leaving to search for the poachers was going to be a hard subject. She will fight me on my decision.

Momma and I prepared breakfast in silence. Once again, we are at odds with our emotions. I decided that the weeks will be even longer if the two of us are not truthful with our feelings.

"Momma, I know you are upset about Father going on the trip. It will be alright."

"Oh, Zura, it's not that."

"Then what is it?" I asked.

"Your father is not feeling well, Zura. He has had some issues for several months. The reason he is going is to see a doctor when he gets there."

"No one thought to tell me? How bad is it? What are his symptoms?"

"His heart. He has had problems for several months and he feels as if it is his heart that is giving him trouble. So, you see, I want him to go. But I am also afraid that he will never come home to us."

I hugged Momma. "Father will be alright. He has to be."

"I hope you are right. I cannot imagine life without him."

"I know, Momma. Do Matt and Tim know?"

"Peter said that he would tell them on the way to the United States."

"Tim and Matt will be sure to get him to the very best doctors. Let's not worry until we know more, alright?"

"You are right. I will keep busy with the children. I promised Olivia that we could bake together tomorrow."

"Can you tend to the children so that I can clean out the stalls and check on the elephants?"

"Of course. Afterward, I will go to the field and study the new bull that has been following the herd. I think he will want to breed with them."

"He better not challenge Kendi. Kendi will teach that new bull a lesson or two."

"Yes, Kendi keeps a distance from the herd, but is always watchful of their movements."

"Alright, we will talk more when I am finished with my chores." I gave Momma a quick hug.

When I entered the barn, I was thankful that Matt and Tim had thought to clean up the blood from the killing. They did a good job of removing the scent of blood in the air. I didn't ask what they'd done with the baby elephant. I really didn't want to know, but I had no doubt that they did the right thing.

I mechanically went through my chores, spent some time outside of the barn with Maji, and watched as Momma played with the children. I felt sad for the anxiety that she must be feeling over Father and decided to fill our days with laughter and fun until he returned.

The next morning, I rose early to see to the chores before the children woke. I used my old flashlight to find my way to the barn. I opened the doors wide. Today was the day to allow the new arrivals to mingle with the other elephants. They must feel as though they are part of a herd. It is imperative to their emotional survival to be accepted by the group. Seven elephants live at the sanctuary and many others have decided to live close by. It is always our intent to rehabilitate and release back to the wild. This introduction is the first step in the process.

I was busy with my work when I realized that the sun had come up and my children would be getting up soon. They would be hungry, so I stopped with the chores and went back to the house.

The screened door creaked its familiar sound when I opened it. Neither Olivia nor Charlie had made their way downstairs. I took a few minutes to peel some fruit and slice the bread that Isabella baked just yesterday.

I could hear Charlie laughing and playing upstairs. His sweet voice carried down to the kitchen. What a happy sound to hear him talking to himself.

"Olivia! Charlie! Come down to eat. Would you like to visit Granny to bake this morning?" I called up the stairs.

Charlie appeared at the top of the steps. Sleep has caused his sandy hair to stand on end. "Granny! I wanna see Granny!" Charlie bellowed.

"You have to eat first. Be careful coming down those stairs. Hold on to the side, Charlie."

"Olivia, come on baby," I yelled.

Olivia did not answer me. She is usually the first to want breakfast unless she isn't feeling well. "Olivia, it's time to get up! Are you feeling alright?" I called and began to climb the stairs.

Scooping Charlie into my arms gets harder as he continues to grow, but I lifted him and steadied him on my hip.

"Olivia honey, are you not feeling well?" I called out to her.

Olivia's bedroom was empty. Her covers were disheveled and are partially lying on the floor. It was a typical scene for Olivia's unkempt room. But there was no sign of her. Jeena and Olivia's favorite blanket were gone as well, so I knew that they were together. I worried that Olivia may have wandered outside again. Because I gave in to letting her sleep with Jeena, there should be no reason for her to wander in the night.

The pit of my stomach began to squeeze with a mother's natural worriment.

I carried Charlie downstairs and out the door to search for Olivia, but she was not on the porch or playing anywhere around the outside of the house.

"Olivia!" I called.

I'd just left the barn, but I reasoned that maybe I didn't hear her sneak in.

I walked back to the barn and I put Charlie down. "Stay here, Charlie," I said. "Olivia, come on. It is time to eat. You don't want to make Granny wait. We are not playing hide and seek right now,"

I said and opened the barn door. It creaked, and glided open with ease. I stepped inside and began to check the stalls. The baby elephant, Maji, two older elephants and Neema were the only inhabitants. There was no sign that Olivia had been in the barn.

My stomach twisted a little tighter and my breath started to quicken. A little bit of parental panic started to set in.

Charlie and I went back into the house to search for Olivia, but it is void of her sounds.

I left Charlie in the living room and raced back up the stairs to see if she had gone into my room to sleep after I awoke. I peeked under my bed. Again, there was no sign of her. She was not in Charlie's room either.

Her room was the last place that I rechecked. I looked under the bed before I sat and tried to calm myself. It became harder to think clearly and keep myself from overreacting.

"Where are you?" I whispered.

As I lifted her cover from the floor, a piece of paper floated to the ground. I grabbed it and read it before I placed it on the bed and began to cry.

We have your child. Come and get her, Jane.

CHAPTER 5

My hands were shaking under the weight of Charlie. I tried to run as fast as I could with him on my hip, yelling for Momma as I ran. Momma's home was only another hundred feet, but my legs wobbled out of fear for Olivia. Adrenaline was the only thing keeping me going.

The porch of my childhood stood in front of me and the stairs seemed impossible to climb, but I could not waste any time. I pushed myself forward, taking two steps at a time. I put Charlie down when I opened the screened door. "Momma! Come quick!" My voice cracked. "Momma! Olivia's missing!" But the house was empty. I knew exactly where to find my mother. For once, I was grateful for her predictability.

I leaned down to Charlie's height. "Let's go for a ride," I said.

Charlie was excited and circled behind me. He grabbed onto my shoulders and I hoisted him up high on my back. We took off running toward the field.

Winded and exhausted, I stopped when I saw her. She was spread out on her blanket with her books and charts, writing something. She stopped only to pause and look back at the herd before making notes again in her book.

I approached her at a brisk walk. Exciting the elephants would not be a wise move.

"Momma," I call out without acknowledgement. "Momma!" I screamed.

"Yes, Zura. I can hear you." She does not look from her book. She just continues to write.

My frustration and fear bubbled to the surface. "Why are you here? I need you!"

Finally, my tone got her attention and she paused to look at her watch. "Zura, it is early. We are not baking for another hour. I just wanted to get some field time before we bake this morning." She looks from me to Charlie. "Where is Olivia? Did she spend the night with the twins? She just loves sleepovers."

I put Charlie down and took his hand in mine. "Momma, Olivia is gone!" I stood over her wanting her concern to match my own.

Momma stood and faced me with a worriment on her face and in her voice that matched my fear. "What? Olivia can't be missing. She is probably playing somewhere with that monkey."

I reached into my pocket and pulled out the note left for me. My shaking hands caused it to flutter out of my grasp.

Momma picked up the note and I watched as her face changed from calm to panic. She quickly began to look in every direction. "Who are they? Why did they take Olivia?"

"I don't know. We must get to Isabella's, Momma. I can get some supplies. I need to find Olivia before it's too late. She does not know how to survive in the jungle like I did." Tears form and slide down my cheeks.

"Yes, of course," Momma answered and wiped a tear with her shaking fingers. She looked down at her things, and for the first time in her life, she walked away from her books and charts and grabbed Charlie from my hand instead. She chose me. She chose her grandchildren over everything else.

Momma looked up at me and swallowed down her own fears. "We will find her. She will be alright, Zura. If anyone in this world can locate her, it is you."

"Mama I'm so scared, what if I can't find her?"

"Zura, you will find her. I have every confidence that you can do this. You have to keep your head. You have to focus. Let's get to Isabella. We will talk through this. It's going to be alright, I just know it. Like I said, if anyone can find her, it's you."

"Thank you, Momma. I won't stop until she is back home with us." I was adamant and the tone of my voice became hardened. *This was not going to happen again. I don't know who they are or what their end game is, but they won't win.* Deep down, however, I was still that scared little girl. And even then, I wasn't as afraid of the outcome as I was right now.

We walked quickly to Tim and Isabella's home. Our hands locked, we ran up to find Isabella knitting on the porch. "Good Morning," she said, not taking her eyes off her work."

"Izzy."

She immediately heard the panic in my voice and dropped the knitting onto her lap. "What is it? What has happened? Is it our men?"

"No. It's Olivia. They have taken her."

"Who has taken her? What do you mean?"

"I handed her the note." Isabella's hand moved to her mouth as she read it. "Oh, Zura. What can I do?"

"Please keep the children together. Momma knows what to do at my barn. Just please take care of Charlie. I am going to get my daughter back."

"Be careful, my Sister. You are the target, not Olivia. She is fine. You have to believe that."

I looked from Isabella to Momma. "If they harm her in any way, I will kill them all."

With the men gone, it was up to me to find my little girl.

Before I left, Isabella placed some food in a small sack that I tied around my waist. I ran back to my home, knowing that Charlie was in good hands. Momma and Isabella would keep him safe.

I grabbed my emergency cloth bag. It had a rope handle so I could easily sling it over my shoulder and carry it on my back. It contained extra clean water in a canteen, matches in a watertight container, binoculars, and just about everything I might need to survive in the jungle, minimally at least. I threw in a clean change of clothes for Olivia and tucked my Smith and Wesson into my belt. I placed a knife in my back pocket and one in my high boots.

I was ready for whatever war I was going to face.

I circled the house and found the answer as to how they entered my home. A ladder from the barn was lying in the grass outside of Olivia's window. Someone climbed up and entered her bedroom while I was sleeping. I wondered, if I am the target, why they just didn't kill me in my sleep. I had a feeling that they have more planned for me than just a quick death.

With no time to lose, I ran to the edge of the jungle and stopped to focus my mind, to attune myself to the vibrations of the earth. They would leave a trail and a scent, and all I must do is follow it.

I was still early morning and the jungle was ominously silent. Nothing stirred beneath my feet. No creatures were scavenging in the dense underbrush. Even the birds' calls could not be heard. The monkeys swayed silently in the trees above my head, but were focused on my every move. I moved quickly, changing my pace from a swift walk, to an all-out run for as long as I could.

The monkeys followed me. There was a time when I would have been excited to see them. I would swing in the trees and race them. I learned how to climb by watching their movements. Imitation is the best form of compliment.

Now that I am an adult, they do not have the same appeal. Although, today they are a reminder of why I am here. My sweet daughter and her monkey are missing; kidnapped from my home. There is nothing in this world that terrorizes my soul greater than something happening to my children.

A panic tear traveled down my cheek and I brushed it away with the back of my hand.

My mood was reflected in my environment; solitude and a deathly stillness. It was so unusually quiet that I could hear my rapid heartbeat pounding in my ears. The steady, quick drumming echoed in my chest; a pulsating sound from within. But I knew one thing for sure. The silence meant the kidnappers were not far. They had passed through here only a short time ago, short enough for the jungle to still be reflecting their presence.

I had to slow my pace before my heart exploded. I tried to focus on the sunlight that poured through small openings in the trees to shine onto the jungle floor. Its warm rays pierce at my back when I stopped to rest calmed me and slowed my heart rate.

I looked at the ground and noticed something shimmering. My locket. The one shaped like a heart that opened and contained pictures of my children. I scrambled over to the locket and picked it up. I unlatched the tiny gold latch on the side of the locket and opened it to see Olivia's dimpled face smiling back at me. She is innocent but strong. Olivia must have taken it like she had so many previous times.

Her fascination with my few items of jewelry was understandable. The stealing is not. For once, I am grateful that she ignored my warning. This time her disregard for my rules told me I am on the right path.

For hours I listened and smelled the air, looking for signs that there had been someone in the jungle. My journey took me to a very dense part of the bush. It felt as though there were many eyes watching me. It could be the monkeys, or it could be the people indigenous to this part of the jungle. I prayed that if it was the people, they would provide me a safe passage through their land. Everything is new and strange to me. I have never spent time in this part of the jungle. Trees are thick with vines and leaves from many different species of plants. It became increasingly harder to follow the path in front of me.

I kept my body low and silently moved in what I determined to be the direction the kidnappers went.

A sudden call from the birds above me, mixed with the scatter of monkeys, told me that I was not alone.

I saw movement on the path in front of me and heard the movement behind me as well. I continued to move slowly, hoping they would simply let me pass.

A bird-like whistle was shared between them and I knew I was surrounded. The narrow passageway was blocked by three native men. In the trees, more men swung to my location and perched in the trees above my head. Behind me, they moved closer and closer until I felt the prick of a wooden spear.

The men wore long skirt-like garments. The material extended up to wrap around their right shoulders. They wore colorful belts and tiny baskets across their bodies. Each man held a spear that was now pointed at me. The men tried to communicate with me in a language that I did not understand.

I remained calm and spoke in Swahili to the men. There was no response.

I tried again, putting my hand to my heart. "Zura. I am Zura."

The men reacted to my name in a panicked tone. They began to speak frantically to each other. The only word I understood was my own name.

One of the men in front of me spoke quickly but I could not understand his words. A man behind me gently pushed me forward and I had no choice but to move in the direction that they commanded. I followed their lead in silence.

We traveled for a long distance through a path that was so well hidden, even I couldn't see it. But the men could. They must know every inch of this part of the jungle. Tracing their steps without hesitation, their unexpected turns took us beyond the heavy vegetation.

Every now and then, I received a slight shove from behind to quicken my pace. I nervously complied. Not that I had a choice.

The tribesmen continued to talk to each other. The only word that I recognized was the continued use of my name. These men know me or know *of* me. I only hoped that it was in a good light.

We continued to walk until, suddenly, the jungle opened up to a hidden village. Grass-thatched roofs on houses made with woven sticks scattered the open borders. Each home had an area for cooking, some with strips of meat drying near the fire. Women were preparing food and weaving grasses, while the children ran and played without fear. A whiff of wild boar mingled with the smell of smoke. The smell reached my nose and my stomach responded in an angry growl. Forgetting to eat does not help my senses.

My eyes drank in the sights. One of the first things that I noticed was that they were a territorial unit that protected their borders. Men sat high in the trees like guardians of the tribe. Other men were returning with food for the tribe.

In the middle, surrounded by others, sat a man I assumed to be their chief. His authoritative posture let me know that he was the man in charge. A frightening black leopard's head adorned him like a crown. Our eyes lock for a second, followed by his whisper into the ear of a man sitting to his left.

Next to this man of power sat a woman that I assumed to be his wife. Several children of different ages surrounded her.

When I was a child, my parents would tell me stories about some tribes deep in the jungle. They were savages that killed their enemies. The tales included poisonous darts, burning the flesh of their victims, dismemberment and other heinous ways to die. Crossing through their lands could make anyone their enemy.

I could never tell if my parents told me these stories because they wanted to frighten me, or if they in fact knew of travelers who never returned from this part of the jungle. I remembered that the most fearsome tribe was the Swavendi people. My father told me one story about how the chief of the Swavendi tribe killed the black leopard, saving his people from slaughter by the man-eating beast.

After seeing their chief, I can only conclude that these are the same people that my parents warned me about in my youth.

The tribesmen led me past several smaller huts grouped together. I took notice of young girls entering one of the huts followed by middle-aged women. I remember hearing stories about the girls sharing a hut at the age of thirteen. The women of the Swavendi people taught the girls about giving birth, motherhood, and how to attend to a husband. The girls are free to talk openly about the changes to their bodies and prepare for their lives as Swavendi mothers. All hoping to become a bride of one of the chief's sons.

Not all of the stories about the people of the jungle were bad. Some were fascinating.

The men who led me to the village shoved me until we stood outside of one of the huts. One of the men pointed for me to enter the shelter.

I leaned down to clear the low doorway and I entered the spacious, single-room hut.

There were two children sitting in the corner that stared at me. They were dressed in the same way as the men but were missing the pouches tied around their waists.

A petite woman entered the hut but avoided eye contact with me. She gave me fruit and cured meat.

An elderly woman then entered the hut with water for me to drink.

I tried speaking in Swahili to thank the women. "Asante," I said, nodding to the women.

They only nodded in reply, avoiding my gaze, and they quickly exited the hut.

The young children followed their lead and ran to the door without a second glance at me.

A young man entered the hut next and sat beside me on a chair. "You are Zura?"

"I am. But how do you know how to speak English?" I ask.

"There have been English travelers who have come to our jungle. Our chief wished for me to learn the language from a scientist who stayed with our tribe for many changing seasons. He studied our people to write about our ways. He is the only traveler that our chief let write our stories."

"Yes, I have heard stories about your people from scientists that have visited us at our home."

"We are the people of the leopard." In many civilizations, the chief is considered a holy man. He and his male offspring protect the people.

This chief wore the head and fur of the black leopard on his head.

"Our chief knows of you. He wants to meet the girl who tamed the wild dog and rides the elephants. He says your heart be true if you tame a mighty hunter, the wild dog, and save it from the leopard. Your soul be white if the elephant loves a little girl enough to save her life. Tell me, Zura of the elephants, are you a shaman? Are you a healer or perhaps a spirit? How do you have such a connection to the animals? Why do they come to your aid?"

His statements shocked me. I couldn't speak; I couldn't think. These people from the jungle know me. They know my story.

"How do you know who I am?"

Everyone know you, Jungle Girl."

For the first time in my life I am not offended by that nickname. They say it with pride and not with sarcasm. "Yes, I am that Jungle Girl that you speak of. I am Zura."

"You are not Jane as the tales of your life says?"

"No, I am not Jane. My name is Zura," I say annoyed by the reference.

The man raised both of his hands to me. "My name is Taji and I do not mean to hurt you, Zura. We have come to know that the men who kidnapped you and held you as a prisoner called you by this name. I mean no disrespect. Our people call you Jungle Girl, Zura, and Jane. Please, I mean no disrespect to you."

Again, I am in awe of this soft-spoken man. "No, I am sorry. It is alright. You can call me any one of the names that you have come to know me by, it's alright," I said.

Taji leaned closer and in almost a whisper he spoke. "Tell me, Zura, what brings you so deep into the jungle? My chief wants to know."

"Taji, it's my daughter. Someone has taken my daughter and I am trying to track them. I am pretty sure they traveled in this direction."

"Yes, we allowed them to travel through our land because they had a small child with them. Tell me, Zura, what is the child's name?"

"Olivia," I said as my voice cracked.

"And these very bad men have taken her from you? Have taken her from her home? Why do they do such a thing?" Taji asks.

"They want me to chase them. They want to kill me."

"You know this, and still you travel alone? Where are the men of your family? Why do they not help you find your child?"

The men have gone to America. The United States."

"They leave the women alone? They all leave? You have no men to protect you, Jane?"

I paused at the use of the name. "No. Yes, I mean. Please, do not call me Jane. That name was used by bad men who taunted me with it when they were trying to kill me. I cannot seem to get over the hate I felt from the men when they used that name."

Taji nodded. "Are you confused about your men leaving?"

"No. Yes, the men left, and yes the women are alone, but the women in my family are sturdy. I am strong and will protect my family."

"Yes, we know that you are a strong girl."

"Then you know why I must travel through your jungle to get to my daughter. Can you help me?"

"I will ask our chief for you, brave Jungle Girl. I will ask for his wisdom on this."

"Please, Taji, with respect, hurry. With every minute that passes the trail grows colder."

Taji stood and slightly bowed to me. "Don't worry, Jungle Girl. If the chief allows us to help you, these men will be found. They cannot hide from us. We know where they have been and can track them easily." He turned and exited the hut. The women returned to check on my water supply and left again.

I was alone in the hut and wasting precious time. The anxiety of waiting made me pace about the room. The entrance to the hut was guarded by two men with spears, and I was unsure whether I am a guest or a prisoner.

I know that I will offend the chief if I try to escape. They may chase me if I flee, so I decided if I wanted their help, I had to stay.

I peeked out of the door every few minutes, looking for the man who speaks English.

As I took notice of the size of the other homes, I realized that this is a larger hut than some of the others. Its thatched roof and wooden walls were very similar to the huts near my home.

Several women entered the hut to bring me food and more water. They tugged and braided my hair into strings. My hair dangled with beads attached to each strand. When they stood back to look at their work, the women giggled and spoke to one another. I did not understand what they were saying as they tugged again at my hair.

Several hours had passed and the sun had set. Finally Taji returned with the answer from his chief.

"Hello, Zura. I am sorry for the long delay. Our chief takes his time when making decisions about the Swavendi. He had to wait for the stars. He has consulted with the stars and has made his decision. The chief says that we can help you to reach your daughter. We can eliminate the men who hold your child.

"That's great! When can we leave? We have to start looking for her right away."

"We cannot leave yet, Zura, there is more to do before we will travel with you."

"What? What needs to be done? I will do it," I said urgently.

"You must become the wife of the chief's son. You must be one with the Swavendi before we put the lives of any of our warriors at risk."

"A wife?" I cannot be the chief's son's wife. I am a married woman."

Taji paused and stared into my eyes before he spoke. "I will tell our chief that you refuse his offer of marriage to his son. He will not be happy that you have rejected his offer. You have refused the stars."

Taji turned to leave and I grabbed his arm. "Wait!"

I heard the drums pounding and I began to sweat. "Taji. Wait, please. Please ask the chief if there is another way to gain his protection. Please, I must keep going. I have to find my little girl."

Taji grabbed my arm. He is locking us in what feels like a handshake. "For you I will ask."

Taji walked to the door, then stopped to turn and look at me. "Jungle girl does not suit you. You should be called Jungle Queen." Taji winked at me with a smile and turned to leave.

I waited several more hours until Taji returned. He had a very serious look on his face that immediately concerned me.

"Zura, we have an answer. You must join our tribe. Our children have been told the story of the animal-taming girl who commanded her animals to kill the bad men in the jungle. They were raised on your story. The chief received a message that your soul is pure, and you are worthy of the title.

You will become Gamba-Fari. It means Warrior Queen."

"I accept!" I said quickly. "Can I go now?"

"No, Gamba-Fari, there must be a ceremony tonight under the fullest moon. Once you are a Swavendi woman, we will—we must—protect you. Our warriors will take you to your daughter and we will kill the men who have hurt you. Your daughter will be under our protection, so long as she is on our lands. We cannot cross over into another tribe's lands, or we start a war."

"Please, I can travel alone."

"We will take you as far as we can go. Until then, you will be spending time getting ready for the ceremony. Our women are wise and have already plaited your hair. They will dress you as one of them for the ceremony, and you will be presented to our chief and our great mother."

"I will be honored," I said, and he took my hand. "You will be the sister of our people, the Warrior Queen. You will have many brothers and sisters to love and protect you and your other family."

I became enamored with the sentiment.

"I will be honored to call you my brother, Taji. Thank you for helping me in my quest."

He took my arm into his hands and squeezed it before he turned to leave the hut.

Several giggling women entered the hut and pulled at my clothes. They carried a beautiful patterned cloth of many colors. The women wrapped it around my body to create a sarong. It was prettier than any that I have seen in the papers that Tim has shipped in from the United States.

A patterned belt was secured around my waist. I felt the finely woven material and knew that great care was taken in making the belt and the cloth.

"It's beautiful," I said to the women.

There is no response as they paint a white line across my forehead and down my cheeks. My lips are painted with a reddish color. Black lines decorate my eyes.

"Thank you," I said quietly.

I must look fierce in my ceremonial outfit.

The women stepped back to look at their work and make a few adjustments before they smiled at me in unison.

They pulled on my arm to follow them.

I left the hut to find Taji waiting outside for me. He was dressed in the same colorful cloth and belt.

There was a woman and three small boys dressed like Taji and me. I guessed them to be his family.

I took notice that each family unit had a different belt. Their belts were a blend of colors similar to Taji's but woven to be a pattern of distinction. It looked as though family units within the tribe were dressed as one.

I take the ends of the belt into my hands to feel the tight woven pattern. "Taji, are these your house colors?"

"Yes," he smiled. "You are very observant. It has done you well in your life, Gamba-Fari. From this day forward, you will be known as my sister, from my father and mother. This ceremony will bind us by blood. We will be one. And your people will protect you. Family units are grouped together. They wear their house colors and patterns with pride. The woven belts and distinct face markings link family members. Some family members are very large, with parents and grown children with their children. You and your family are now of my house."

I had a sudden urge to hug Taji, but I wasn't sure whether it would be appropriate.

Taji saw it in my eyes and smiled. "There is a lifetime to know you and your family, my sister."

"From being an only child, I now have two brothers. I am blessed," I said.

"It is true that your Tim is every bit your brother as I will be."

Standing next to Taji, I noticed how much taller I was than the Swavendi. It is no wonder that they see me as a warrior.

Taji took my arm and led me to the rest of his family, and he stood proudly next to his wife. "This is my wife, Imani."

"I am pleased to meet you," I bow ever so slightly.

Imani was beautiful. She was dressed similar to the other women. Her garment wrapped tightly around her chest, a modesty that is unlike other tribes. Her hair was plaited in thin, rope-like strings that extend down her back. Imani's hair was colored to resemble the rich, clay grounds, with a hint of red that matched the skies just before the sun sets. Her eyes were big and dark when they stared into mine. Her lips were perfectly shaped and her smile was genuine. Imani had a fuller figure. It is a sign of her fertility, which is what the African men look for in a wife and mother of their children.

I could see by the way that Taji looked at his wife, that he knew that he had selected wisely. I imagine he is envied by other men who could have wanted her as a wife.

Imani spoke in a soft whisper for only her husband to understand.

Taji translated for me with a smile on his young handsome face. "Imani says a queen bows to no one."

I recognized Imani as one of the women that helped to get me ready for the ceremony. Her dark face is painted like mine, in deep yellow shades that suit her beautiful skin. She spoke to Taji who laughed before he translated her message.

"Imani says welcome to our family. It is good luck to have the animal tamer on our side."

Her kind eyes expressed no judgement. She spoke to Taji again.

"Imani says that she would personally kill the people that have taken your child. They are evil and will pay for upsetting the stars."

"Taji, please tell her that they will pay dearly for upsetting the stars and taking my child."

Imani nodded with my answer and placed her hand on my arm.

Taji placed a hand on the shoulder of one of the boys standing next to him. "We have three children, all boys, named Ade, Salim, and Abayomi. Imani wants a daughter soon, so we will keep trying," he chuckled.

I smiled at the children whose heights differed with their ages. "Hello," I said to the stone-face boys. They stared at me as if they were fearful and remained silent.

Taji motioned me forward. "Come and sit beside me to watch the bridal ceremony."

"Who is getting married?" I asked.

"Our chief Kimoni's son. It is soon time for our chief to leave us and live with our ancestors. His son, Abioye, will become our new chief. So, it is time for Abioye to choose a wife. This bridal ceremony will reveal her to him and if she agrees, she will be the wife of his choosing.

"She has a say in it?"

"Of course. It is her decision. Because every family wants to be connected to the chief, it is unlikely that any of them will say no. It will be an honor to her family to become part of Kimoni's family and give birth to a future chief to follow Abioye's rule."

"Abioye will just know?" I asked. "I have heard of this ceremony and I'm excited to watch the process. What of the women who are not selected?"

I'd heard other stories or legends about ceremonies among the tribes. Like the one about the wife ceremony; also called the dance of the python. It is said that the men and women link arms to form a snake-like pattern in the middle of the ceremonial circle. They dance to the music of the drums, moving and gyrating their bodies to resemble the movements of the snake. It isn't until the eldest son of the chief chooses his wife that the chain is broken.

This starts the mating time period that can last several days before the marriage ceremony is performed by the chief.

I looked around to see men making musical instruments out of bamboo.

Another legend is that the young men of the Swavendi travel to a very remote area of the jungle to choose their bamboo. Not every young man returns from the journey. This is the ritual to manhood within the tribe.

A ceremony is held when the young men return. They create their musical instruments out of the bamboo and play their instruments during the celebration. Others dance to the music out of celebration for their passage into manhood.

The dancing and activities created an atmosphere full of happiness and the coupling of the young girls to the mate of her choosing. But I was getting anxious about Olivia. Almost an entire day had passed since she'd been taken. I knew I could have tracked the men who took her, but what if they greatly outnumbered me? That's why I stayed. To enlist the help of the Swavendi. I'd have to politely wait it out.

The tales of the Swavendi are exciting to me. If I had more time, I would naturally want to learn more. But time is the one thing I don't have.

"The young men will also be looking for their wife, so you might see some of them become a couple during the ceremony. You will not only watch but be a part of it. It will take the spirit of the tribe to help Abioye make the right decision."

"He will just know?" I repeated.

"He will know tonight who the heavens say is his mate, yes."

The tribe formed a large circle around a fire, with each family sitting together. I watched as Kimoni sat on a stool to be higher than the rest of his people. Abioye took a seat to his right. The rest of the family encircled them to show unity. This process continued within each family. The males are encircled by the women and their children.

"Taji, that is interesting that the men are in the circle surrounded by their women. I guess that it is showing the importance of males in your culture."

"I suppose that you might see it that way."

"That's not the way it is?"

"Oh, yes, our men are strong hunters and protect their family. Our women protect our men. Our women are strong, and they make sure that their men do not go without food to strengthen their bodies. They clothe their men and weave our ancient family symbols. The women care for and nurture our children. They are the fierce protectors of their family. Our women are selfless and are adored by their husbands. Do you understand this?"

"Oh, yes I suppose that my family unit is very similar. Our husbands make our houses and tend to the protection of our families. They are forever acting against anything that may harm us. Our women make the home and feed and tend to our children. Well, except my husband Matt. He equally tends to our children."

"How many children do you have?"

"Two. Olivia, she is my oldest. She is six. My youngest is Charlie. Charlie is two. He is with my sister-in-law."

"What is "in-law"? Is she not your sister?"

"She is married to my brother, Tim. That makes her my "in-law". We are very close, and I think of her as my sister." I smiled thinking of Isabella. "We call her Izzy. She is an excellent mother. I hope to be like her one day."

"My sister, you are also a fierce protector of your family. Look how far you have come. You will stop at nothing to get your child back. Your new name suits you, Warrior Queen."

"Thank you, Taji, for everything. I will forever be grateful for your help."

Now that the people had gathered, the drums began to beat again. Slowly and softly they started to build.

Small children stood and placed small taro roots on a pile in the middle of the circle.

"This is a sign of strength in our children. They have selected and pulled the root of a new tree," Taji explained.

More and more taro roots were piled into the center of the circle by slightly older male youths. The drums began to increase in intensity and young men stood and started to dance around the root pile. It was like they were hopping and then bowing to the women on the other side of the circle.

"These men present larger taro roots that they have dug up, it is a sign of strength. The larger the root, the stronger the warrior." Taji says. "Older boys that are old enough to take a mate dig up large Taro and carry it into the circle on long sticks."

I watched the men proudly dance in the middle of the circle.

Older men dig up yams and danced with them in the center before placing them on the pile of growing food.

Taji motioned for me to look as a dead pig was carried into the circle. "A pig that was raised by the son of the chief is slaughtered and sectioned off and given to each mother of a family."

The circle widened and the males and females old enough to mate formed a line in the middle of the circle. They joined arms with the person in front and behind them, making a long chain. Abioye sat next to his father and mother. He yelled for the music to start and the chain of people began to dance and gyrate their bodies. They raised and lowered their joined hands as they moved in a large circle. The movement resembled a snake slithering as they glided their bodies as one. Abioye paid very close attention for several minutes. He then rose and broke the chain to remove one beautiful young girl.

She had yellow stripes across her face to resemble a tiger. Her tiny waist and larger hips are a sign of her fruitfulness. She nodded at Abioye and they were promised to one another.

I turned to Taji. "What is her name? She is beautiful!"

"Her name is Oshun. Yes, she comes from a very beautiful family."

"What happens next?" I asked.

"Others in the circle will now pick mates. The men will approach the women and they will shake or nod their heads. Some will become a couple, and some will not."

"This is fascinating to me. Tell me more about these rituals. What happens after the couples are coupled?"

"The young girls will leave their families and join each other in the courting huts. This is where their mothers and other women from the tribe will teach them how to tend to a family. They learn about birthing children and sex. After they have learned what the women can teach them, each girl that will soon become a wife will have a courting hut for private dinners and time to be alone with their soon-to-be-husbands."

The beauty of the ceremonies, the openness and support that these young women receive from their mothers and other women astonished me. Momma's explanation of the passage into womanhood was a scientific explanation of fertilized eggs, embryos, and a dissertation of genetics.

Taji spoke softly as the drums subsided.

"Before the wedding, the brides will be painted with henna. Somewhere on their bodies, her husband's name is hidden. On their wedding night, it is up to the husband to find his name. It signifies her passage to womanhood and fertility."

"That is beautiful, Taji."

"Our women are beautiful. We cherish them."

"What happens next?"

Taji looked at me and then at Kimoni. The chief nodded his head. Taji looked back at me. "It is time for you to take your place within the tribe."

I felt a nervous knot in my stomach. Unaware of what I will have to do, I followed Taji to the circle.

All at once, everyone adorned their family masks. Looking around me, I could see elaborately painted disguises through the fire.

Taji placed a beautifully carved, wooden black mask on his face. It was a long, shiny cat-like design with pointy ears. The eyes were yellow, along with the eyebrows. It resembled part human, part cat.

"What does this mask mean?"

"It is our belief that humans can transform into animals. It is our way to our ancestors to ask for guidance and approval. We only use our family masks during special times such as this. Look and you will see masks of the elephants, lions, buffalo and even monkeys. These masks transform us into our spirit animals. We are of the black leopard family."

"Just like the chief?"

"Yes, we are related," Taji said. "Tonight, you will become your spirit guardian during the ceremony. The transformation will make you feel as though you are passing through the stars and leaving this earth. Listen to the messages from the other side. They will give you the wisdom that you will need to make this journey."

"The other side?" I asked. "The other side of what?"

"You will leave your body and fly to the stars to be given your message."

I didn't believe what Taji was telling me, but I would never disrespect him by telling him of my doubts. I remained silent and focused on the masked people that surround me.

He laughed when he looked at my face. "You will see, Gamba-Fari. You will see," he said as he handed me a similar mask.

I held the disguise to my face and peered out of the eye holes.

Taji touched my mask. "These were carved by the males in my family when they were just boys. When we are welcomed to manhood, we must go into the jungle and find the wood that we will use. We pass them onto our family members. This mask was carved by my brother, Baako. He was a fierce protector of our family and has been gone for three years now."

Oh, I am sorry, Taji."

"Do not feel sad for those who pass on to the ancestors. They have no troubles, no hurt. They live in peace and happiness to watch over us from the skies. Be happy for their wisdom in the messages we receive. They guide our family to the answers to their heart's questions."

"That is a lovely way to look at death."

"It is our belief. It is the way we live. I do miss our hunting together and his friendship."

"If you don't mind. How did he die?" I asked.

"He was killed by a local tribe that said he passed onto their lands. They say he knew where our land ends and he crossed to their land to kill the animals in their territory. He was killed by a poisonous dart. It killed him almost instantly. My brother was a fine man and protector of his family.

I was speechless and honored to wear the mask of Taji's brother at the ceremony.

The people now stood and began to bounce to the quickening beat of the drums.

Taji smiled at me. "Listen to the sound of the drums. They will lead you on your journey to receive your message."

I could feel all the eyes of the tribe on me. It made me a little bit nervous about what was about to happen.

Imani took the mask from my hands and motioned for me to bend. She tied the mask around my head and without hesitation, she took my left hand.

Taji stood to the right of me and linked his hand in mine. Together, they led me to Kimoni, united with me. Just like that, they welcomed me into their lives.

I stood before the Swavendi chief with nothing to offer him.

Kimoni stared at me as I stared at him through the eye slits in the mask. The black leopard on Kimoni's head looked like it could spring at me and bite my face with those sharp fangs.

It felt like several minutes passed before he spoke. His voice carried on the sound of the drums in an authoritative speech, loud enough for everyone to hear him.

Taji translated his words for me. "Kimoni says, Gamba-Fari stands before us ready to take the family vow. Taji, her brother will unite Gamba-Fari to his family. She will seek the wisdom of the ancestors and travel to the skies." Kimoni raised his hands above his head and began a song. The tribe joined him, matching the beat that started low and slowly built to a quicker pace filled with energy.

Taji pulled out a knife with a braided leather handle. The blade resembled a hand-carved stone. "Put both of your hands out in front of you with your palms up, Gamba-Fari."

I placed my hands in front of me as he instructed, and he put the primitive-looking knife handle across my palms. He placed both of his hands flat onto mine with the knife between us and applied pressure, intertwining our fingers.

Taji's smiling eyes peered into mine. "By family, by blood, we are united. Your name within our tribe will forever be Gamba-Fari, the Warrior Queen. Our family is strengthened with your power and love. We are united by body, by heart, by blood." Taji lifted his hands and looked intently into my eyes. "Do not flinch, do not move. This will show your commitment and the strength you bring to the tribe."

Taji took my right hand and sliced the knife gently through my palm. I stayed completely still to the pain and sight of my blood flowing from the wound. Taji nodded and smiled. He sliced his hand and placed our palms together, mingling our blood. "We will forever be as one family. My blood is your blood. Your blood is my blood, until death, my sister."

He raised our joined hands high above our heads and the tribe ignited into shouts and celebratory singing.

Kimoni handed Taji a spear and the beat accelerated.

Taji handed the spear to me then left me alone in the circle. He joins his wife and children.

A separate fire was lit. Women entered the circle with large wet leaves and placed them on the fire. Other grasses and foreign plants were placed on the burning leaves.

Quickly, the smell permeated the air with a sweet, rich scent mingled with the burning wood and leaves. Gray and white smoke slowly danced skyward, thickening the air around me. Tendrils of smoke made their way into my lungs and caused my mind to cloud with the humid night air.

Just when I thought I would suffocate from the smoke, the tribe's people began to come nearer to me. The circle was closing around me. The hum of the beat mingled in the cloudy air.

The hands of every close tribe member touched my relaxing body. My arms, my shoulders and back were supported by my extended family.

Taji whispered in my ear. "Feel the energy and let your mind go with the spirit of the smoke. Become one with the song and the people who give you their liveliness."

The singing, the drums, and the tribe's buzzing energy made me feel extremely light-headed. The tribe began to slowly and gently push on my body. They lulled me into some sort of trance. I swayed and spun, letting go of my mind. The humming from the tribe was both soothing and mesmerizing. I felt myself slipping, falling into nothingness.

When I opened my eyes, I saw nothing. I was alone in the dark. Somehow the darkness was soothing with the black hues that gave way to a growing light that approached me.

A cooling breeze touched my skin, leaving a shiver of freshness on my flesh.

There was a gentle whisper in the air, like the sound of a man whose words are inaudible. The murmur grew in my ears. I could not be sure of the source of the sounds, but it seemed to be coming from the growing yellow-white light that began to shift its shape. I saw a lion, then a tiger. The giraffe appeared and morphed into a black leopard surrounded by the light. It moved in almost a stalking gate before it stood on its back legs. The morphing continued until there was a man before me.

His resemblance to Taji was remarkable, though I couldn't see through him. Not a mortal form, he was more like an impression or replication of the man I knew.

The form whispered to me in the language of his people.

I listened intently as his words were translated on the air.

"She will not be harmed. You are his enemy. He has waited a lifetime driven by revenge. He seeks your blood, your death and will not stop until he drinks it."

"Who is he? Why does someone want me dead? I do not understand."

The spirit avoided my question and continued with his message.

"There is another that you hold dear. He calls out to you. You must act quickly before it is too late."

"Who, who calls out? Is it my husband? Is it my father or brother? Who calls out? Please, I need more information."

My perspective distorted when the light began to fade. With it, so do the answers to my questions.

I felt myself begin to fall. The blackness blurred with the swirling movements of my body. The descent seemed inevitable. I felt that I would not survive the fall.

Spinning and twirling, I had no control but did not feel myself to be in any real danger; I found myself flying above the earth, able to witness all its splendor. The rotation of the earth spinning below me was ever so slight. I saw what Africa looks like on a map that my father hung on the wall of his office. I have traced its lines with my finger as a child.

I knew that I must make my way back to my reality in order to face the person that wants to kill me. I plunged myself downward into blackness.

Someone shook me back from my dream-like state.

"Gamba-Fari, wake up!" Taji tapped my face until I woke.

"What happened?" I tried to focus though the dizziness.

Taji grabbed my arm and lifted me from the jungle floor. "You have received the answer to your questions, Gamba-Fari. What did our ancestors tell you?"

"I saw him, Taji. I saw your brother."

"Yes, I know."

"How do you know? How could you know?" I asked.

"He is your blood now, your brother in the heavens."

"He said that I am the target, not Olivia. That someone wants me dead and will not stop until he drinks my blood. Is that literal? Someone would want to drink human blood? I have heard stories about people who do it, and of course there are cannibals."

"I believe it is not meant in the physical sense. Its meaning is to cause your death," Taji squeezed my arm for support.

I grabbed his arm to stop shaking and stabilize myself.

"You must take it slow, Gamba-Fari. Do not move quickly until the spinning disappears."

"I've never experienced anything like that. I don't think I want to ever again," I said. "He also said that someone else is in danger. I do not know who he was referring to. The only men I think it could be are my father, Tim, or my husband, Matt."

There is another that I cannot imagine ever losing. "Oh, please don't let it be my son, Charlie. Tell me that he is alright!" I grabbed Taji by both shoulders to steady myself.

"Gamba-Fari, we can try to find out what the message means. Tomorrow, we can call upon the spirits to answer your questions."

"Taji, I cannot stay. I must leave at dawn to find Olivia. I have to go."

"Of course." Taji nodded. "We will take you as far as we can travel."

I lay on a woven grass mat in Taji's hut. His family surrounded me as if I belonged. They were kind enough to share their home with me.

The sounds of their sleep, the heaviness of their breathing reminded me that sleep never comes easy for me. I was afraid to close my eyes. I feared the message that replayed in my mind. The images of darkness and the changing of forms from animal to a spirit. The thought of losing someone that I love.

I made myself focus on something other than the message.

I could barely see through the dimness of the hut. There were slight gaps in the walls that caused the tiniest bits of light from the fire to shine and dance into the hut. I traced the light in my mind as it moved and flickered in the darkness.

The absence of light reminded me of the fear inside of me. A small flicker of brightness, the courage to face death for the love of Olivia brightened my path to her freedom. Nothing will break me from this path. I will defend my family and find my daughter.

Just like this family, just like this hut that is strong and sturdy. It's made of strong trees, mud from the very ground it sits upon and the grasses that grow here. It shelters the people.

Taji protected me by making me a member of his family.

Thoughts of Taji and Imani reminded me that they have less than I do, and they have everything they will ever need. The families of the tribe are strong, and they cherish tradition and the bond of their blood.

Even as the sun began to rise, there was no sleep for me. There will be time to rest after Olivia is found and safe in my arms.

Taji and Imani stirred from their sleep. Their boys woke and raced one another out the door, leaving it ajar. Without being told, they gather wood for a fire. Imani gathered large leaves and began to assemble a meal for her hungry brood.

Taji and I were alone in the hut. "I thank you, brother, for being so generous to me."

Taji nodded and smiled at me. "I have also received a message from my deceased family. Their message to me was that I would meet a warrior who needs my help. I must do everything I can to help her on her quest."

"Really, your message was that clear?"

"Yes. It was given to me by my brother. He looks out for me."

"I saw him too."

"Yes, he is a strong spirit that watches over us."

"What other messages have you received from him about me?" I asked.

"The rest is not for you to be concerned. I have made many plans for the rest of my message and I proudly do this for you, Warrior Queen. You must rest, even for a short time. You will need your strength."

"I will try," I answered.

Taji left me alone in the hut. I lay down on the mat and closed my eyes. In the almost silence, I felt myself drifting within minutes. I fell asleep to the light sounds of drums beating in the distance.

Dreams began to haunt me.

I could see a fire and hear the clapping of hands in a slow beat. I was in a circle of masked people that slowly came toward me. They closed in around me. The chanting was more like a hum, whispering softly to me. I wore the black mask of the leopard and danced around the fire with the people of the Swavendi tribe. They are my people.

A man dressed in a beaded chest piece, with thin strips of grasses as his groin covering, stood in front of me.

His mask was long and decorated with black, yellow and orange patterns in the form of a giraffe. Two horns poked from the top of the mask to resemble the horns of the giraffe, but they were much longer. He removed his mask to reveal his tattooed face. His white eyes set against a background of the dark tattoo colors *scared me for a moment. I stepped back from him, running into the tribe people behind me. His pupil-less gaze saw through to my quickly beating heart.*

"Do not be afraid" I am of a tribe family, Gamba-Fari. You are protected by the people. I know you are troubled in your mind. How can I help to calm you before your trip? You travel to your daughter as you face death. You must be strong."

"My death?" I swallowed hard. "Someone else? Do you know?" I asked the illusion. "Tell me about the death. Please do not let it be my daughter."

"I do not see the death of your daughter. She will grow to be as powerful, if not more powerful than you."

My hands flew to my chest in a panic. I tried to touch him but my hand slipped through his image. "Who? Who will die? Is it my son,

Charlie? Please don't let it be him." My heart began to race and my breath came in panicked gasps, even in my sleep.

"Your son lives to be very old."

"Is it my husband, Matt? Is it him?"

"No, your husband will grow old with you, Gamba-Fari."

"Tim or my father? I can't take this guessing game. Tell me what I need to know. Is it one of them?"

The image before me began to fade.

"Stay! Please stay! Answer me!" I yelled and the last thing I saw were his white-filmed eyes as they faded to nothingness.

I bolted upright covered in sweat and yelling. "Wait! Answer me!"

Taji came to me and grabbed my flailing arms. "Gamba-Fari, please. Calm yourself. This is not good for you and your heart. Tell me, what troubles your dreams," he says calmingly.

"I had a vision of a man in a giraffe-shaped mask."

"Giraffe? Are you sure?"

"Very sure. His eyes were colorless, and they frightened me."

"What did he say?"

"He was giving me a message. He told me that one of my family members is in trouble. I was asking about my brother and father and he faded before I could get him to answer. How can I get him back?"

"It is beyond the dawn. We will be leaving. Do not worry yourself about this message. All will be revealed when it is meant for you to know."

"But I have to know what will happen to my family."

"You will, when it is time."

"I don't have time."

CHAPTER 6

There is little light in the thickness of this part of the jungle. Thin scatters of reflections, like heavenly beams show scarcely on the jungle floor.

Vines wrap tightly to the trees that grow to great heights. The nurtured climbers stretched and slithered to the next tree with their thick, snake-like foliage. They are rooted deep and tethered undisturbed by man or creature. The vines silently conquer and survive.

The humid air was dense and suffocating. My lungs felt restricted, as though I was carrying a heavy object on my chest, making them attempt to expand past their capabilities. The weight of the steamy stillness slowed my pace.

So deep into the moistness, a large swarm of mosquitoes infested the air, hanging there in a tight swarm, waiting to find some exposed skin. The men that traveled with me are immune to them. I am not, so they swarm above me and dive at my head, neck and legs.

We had set out at dawn, just as the light of the sun made itself visible over the huts. There was already much activity when I finally got up to join the tribe. I was ready to leave. I needed to leave.

Before we left the village, Taji assembled seven men to join us. They would stay with me through the deepest part of the journey but would stop before passing onto the lands of another tribe. I'd already lost almost two days, but I was confident that the kidnappers—whoever they were—would leave a strong trail for us to follow. They may be ruthless, but I think they would have a more difficult time covering their tracks with a small child in tow. I prayed that Olivia was okay. She's strong and adventurous, even defiant, but she's still a child.

The men carried their spears and poisonous darts for protection. They looked fierce with their red-clay-painted faces. One side of their face was adorned with large white spots, the others side with a yellow, creating the pattern of the giraffe. The giraffe patterns reminded me of the dream and the warning from the man who said that one of my family members was in trouble.

I too am painted, though I wear my regular clothes.

Imani painted my face and neck black. She added a yellow color around, above and below my eyes. She spoke to me as she painted. Taji translated her words for me. "Imani paints your mask. She says that the black leopard will protect you from the dangers of the men and jungle. You will be one with the leopard and he will recognize you as a child of the jungle. He will not harm you or your child."

"Imani is saying that I will see a black leopard?"

"Yes, Imani sees the messages from the stars. She can see the future. She too has dreams."

I stared at the beautiful Imani before I asked. "The rest of the men are painted in the pattern of the giraffe. Why?"

Because the family of the giraffe are our fierce protectors of the tribe. They know the jungle like no other. And the spirit of the giraffe came to you in your dream."

Single file, we moved quietly, trying to remain silent through the dense bush. Heavy vines and thick plants covered the trail from my view. The terrain made our traveling very slow.

Taji found a slightly trodden path. "They have been here," he announced. "These tracks are made from men in boots. They are about a day old, but we can follow them."

I pushed past the men in front of me to see the footprints. A little bare foot print was visible in the soft, wet mud. I leaned down to touch the track made by Olivia and forced back my feelings.

Taji stopped and looked at the trees. He made clicking sounds with his mouth and a soft whistle toward the sky. Well-hidden scouts appeared in the trees. Their camouflage was so good that I would have passed them without ever seeing them.

He motioned for the men to come down and join us. The scouts effortlessly climbed down the trees and greeted Taji with a clasp of their arms. Taji and the guards spoke in their native tongue. When the speech grew louder and quicker, I saw one of the men bring his hands to his mouth, and then he brought his hands together in front of his body.

There is nothing I can do but patiently wait for them to finish before I start to question Taji.

The other scout joined in the conversation, pointing at the trail.

Taji turned to face me and the men that accompanied us.

My anxiety rose, and I could not wait a moment longer. "Did they pass through here? That's Olivia's print, right?"

"Yes, they traveled through here."

"When?"

"They were here yesterday morning."

There were three men, a woman, and a child. She was in the middle of the group."

"Three men and a woman?" *But that would mean that Alex, Alice and his two henchmen never went on the trip back to the United States. How can that be? I thought.*

"Is she alright? Was she crying?" I asked.

Taji hesitated. He avoided my gaze and paused before answering my questions. "No, she was not crying. The men say she is very brave. They say there was a vervet monkey sitting on her shoulder. The child had a blanket wrapped around her."

"What else? What else did they say?"

Taji lifted his head and met my growing anxiousness with a calm gaze. "Gamba-Fari, her mouth is covered with some sort of material, and her hands are tied in front of her."

"No. There was no reason for them to tie her. She is only six years old. She could never escape them."

"I know that your story is the same. I know when you were a child, those men tied you. This must be very hard. But you will help her. Stay focused, Gamba-Fari."

"Why didn't they help her?" I pointed to the tribesmen in anger. "Why didn't your men take her from them?"

"That is not the men's responsibility. They only look for signs of danger for our people. Now that you are of the tribe, they would have taken her from the men for you, and protected her, because she is now one of our people. But the strangers passed through here before you became one with our tribe. Our tribesmen did not see them as a threat to our people when they were traveling away from our village."

"But why was I apprehended as I passed through your lands? Why were they not also taken to the tribe?"

"Because you are the Jungle Girl. It is Kimoni who decides."

I cannot get past the thought of Olivia's hands tied and her little sweet mouth gagged. "They have tied my child. I have to get to her right now. I will kill every one of them if they have hurt her. Taji, we must find Olivia. I have lost too much time."

"You have gained a tribe in that time. We will find her, and we will deal with the men who have taken your daughter, Gamba-Fari. I promise you."

Taji spoke to the men again and they scurried up the trees to continue their turn as guardians.

With a bird-like whistle to the men, Taji motioned that our journey would continue. He led us further into the depth of foliage and vines. The path continued to a water source that was fresh and clean. We paused only to gather water.

The small path continued for several hours until we reached the border of the next tribe—the Ziurxu tribe.

Taji and his men stopped.

"The Ziurxu watch us from the trees to see whether we will cross into their land. We must not travel into their part of the jungle or we risk starting a war for our people against the Ziurxu. Please understand, Gamba-Fari."

"Taji, you have been such a great brother to me. Yes, please stay on your land and do not risk war for your people. I appreciate all that you have done for me and my daughter. I will find them from here."

The sun was now high in the sky. I knew I could travel faster alone, but the tribes were increasingly territorial, much more than when I was a nonthreatening child. I could not afford to be captured and delayed again. "Here." Taji handed me his spear. "The Ziurxu will respect that you have traveled onto our lands and we have not harmed you. I am sure they have seen the men with the child and will know you are here to save her. They will let you pass. Just you. Go now, Warrior Queen, go and find your little one. Kill if you must. They have caused crime against you and your family."

I can only nod and hug Taji before I slipped into the leaves.

They were only a day's time ahead of me. I quickened my pace. I ran and jumped over downed trees. The path was slight, but my tracking senses had fully kicked in and made it easier to see the trail. It wasn't difficult, and almost as though they wanted to leave a trail for me to follow. I needed to be vigilant, wary, and on my guard. If they were expecting me to follow them, the element of surprise would be difficult to maintain.

An hour of running made my side cramp. I slowed the pace and concentrated on the passing light. Nighttime and darkness were approaching, and the dangers of traveling in the dark worried me.

Following the signs of the kidnappers had distracted me from my surroundings until the blood in the air stopped me. Death was close. I grasped harder on the spear.

With a growl so deep it rumbled inside me, a black leopard came out of the bushes and leapt into a nearby tree. His powerful jaws lifted his kill and he slung the lifeless remains over a branch. The dead impala's head hung awkwardly over the limb. His legs jutted out in hard stiff appendages. Flies did not waste time and they began to cover the dead carcass, only to be shooed away with the leopard's bites. The great cat did not see me as much of a threat, but he did hiss at me and I backed away, careful to not take my eyes off him.

He ripped at the impala's flesh with his sharp teeth but followed my movements with his keen yellow eyes.

When I knew that it was safe to turn and walk away, I moved at a steady pace, then ran steadily on until I felt as though I could not run another step.

I propped the spear against a tree. I didn't know what their destination was and I couldn't risk them getting on a prop plane or being met by a motor vehicle. I would lose them completely if that happened and it could happen at any hour. It was time to speed up my movements. I took to the trees.

I picked a tree with low branches and reached high to wrap my hands around the lowest branch. My foot swung naturally to help pull myself up to sit on the limb. Slowly and steadily, I climbed until I was hidden in the leaves. My skills for moving from one tree to the next were shaky from lack of practice, but I managed not to fall. My only focus was getting to Olivia and rescuing her from harm.

After about an hour, my hands and feet moved as they did in my youth, harmoniously swinging and gliding my movements forward. The moon was on my side, full and bright, lighting the sky and giving me the advantage I needed to move through the impending darkness.

My arms began to feel the fatigue from many hours in the trees and exhaustion made by hands shake. I knew they would stop for the night. We had seen evidence of their camp from the night before. Now I had made at least several hours advance on them by continuing long after darkness had descended on the jungle floor.

I settled on a large limb and perched myself for a rest. It would be a mistake to stop for too long. I could not allow the men to maintain a huge gap between us. I plotted my path and pushed on, taking pictures with my eyes to remember the way back out of this part of the jungle.

The trails would be naked to most people's eyes. The slight indentation in the leaves, the sparse growth of vines that had been removed, and the disturbances in the ground were all trail markers to a tracker.

After about another hour I stopped to rest again. My hands were blistering from the bark's roughness. My knees were scraped, but my pride and determination were intact. I remembered what it took to be fluent in the jungle's trees. Slowly, it came back to me. The keen vision and hearing from my youth.

In the darkening jungle, I caught a scent in the air. The odor of wood smoke. And a man's voice. A voice I've never heard before. It's not Alex's boisterous voice or either of his men. He is someone new.

I stopped suddenly when I heard the angry words from a woman. It's Alice's voice, clear as day. Baffled and confused, I continued closer to their fire. The nearer I got, the clearer I could hear their conversation.

"Stop it, Dix!" Alice complained. "She's just a little girl."

"Relax, Alice baby, we ain't gonna hurt her yet. I just don't want her screamin' out for her mommy before we can get ready for the jungle girl to find us, that's all."

"Dix, there is no way she could have reached us already. We left in the middle of the night. She probably slept for hours after that before realizing the kid was missing."

"No, I watched her for a few days. I don't think that one ever sleeps. She's always awake and sitting on her porch. She looks out into the jungle like a big cat looking for a meal. Always ready to pounce."

"I don't understand your fascination with her," Alice pouted.

The man chuckled. "What are you jealous of, the jungle girl? Trust me, doll, it ain't because I have the hots for her. I want her dead. I've always wanted her dead. And now that she's so close, I am finding it hard to control the urge to kill her early. But I want her death to be slow and painful. A slice for every year that he never came home. Maybe even make her watch as I take a slice or two out of her daughter."

I climbed silently closer to get a better look. The leaves hid me from their view, but I saw the back of Olivia sitting on the ground across from Alice. Her shoulders moved with her crying. Jeena sat on her shoulder and nestled in Olivia's hair. She was still wearing her white night dress. Olivia's hands were tied in front of her and there was a rag tied around her head to cover her mouth. It is just like the tribesmen told Taji.

It took all my strength to sit there quietly and not reach for my girl. I wished I still had the spear. I would swing down and run the spear into the hearts of all of them.

My heart was breaking watching Olivia cry, unable to reach her. I have always been the one to dry her tears, to hug away her pains. But this time I needed to stay as still as I possibly could, to ensure that they did not know my location. I was very fearful that they might hurt her. Olivia was already a pawn in this dangerous game.

Taking in the entire scene and looking for as much information as I could was my skill.

The man that was speaking had a hat that shielded his face, so I couldn't identify him.

The other two men I recognized as the guards that accompanied Alex to our home. I wondered what role Alex had in this.

When the man spoke, he had the same accent as Alex and Alice.

Thoughts of Alex's motivation and his role in this were not clear. Was he the diversion? Was it his job to lead me out of the country so that these men could kill me? Did I send my husband, brother, and father into danger by insisting that they go to the United States in my stead?

My mind raced through the information, looking for answers to questions that I probably didn't really want to know. I stopped the thoughts to focus on Olivia and getting her to safety. The rest could be handled when she was safe.

Alice stood and circled to the other side of the fire to sit between Olivia and the stranger. He never turned to look at her. He remained focused on the flames. Olivia's whimpering pulled him out of his trance. "Alice, shut the kid up before she alerts something big to our location. I'm okay with her making noise during the day when we can see what's coming at us, but we don't want any undue attention during the night. Shut her up before I do."

Alice rubbed Olivia's head. "Now Dix, that's no way to talk. She's only a kid. She can't help but be scared. Why she's probably never been away from her mommy. Olivia leaned into Alice for comfort. Alice sat up straight. She looked as though she had never comforted a child before and appeared torn between helping Olivia and her loyalty to the strange man. "It's a good thing you brought that blanket with you and the monkey. Why don't we lay it out and you take a rest right here beside me, okay?" Alice said.

Olivia nodded while she looked around to take in her surroundings. She spotted my location and suddenly our eyes locked. I immediately brought my finger to my lips as a sign for her to be silent. She slowly nodded and lay on the blanket with Jeena snuggled in tight. I moved up into the leaves for better camouflage.

Alice rubbed Olivia's head. "Now isn't that better. You rest now, and in the morning things will be better."

The man chuckled to himself. "They sure will be. I figure if we stay right here, Zura or Jane or whatever her name is will come for the child and I will get the revenge that I have waited for all of my life."

"Are you sure you want to do this, Dix?"

"I've never been more sure of anything in my life. Hardy, you take the first watch and Griffin, you take the second watch in three hours. I will take the watch after both of you."

Alice cleared her throat. Mr. Hardy McBride, you should be careful with that whiskey. You too Mr. Griffin Stone. Don't go drinking all night until you pass out and leave us vulnerable to whatever predators are out there just waiting to make us their next meal.

Hardy let out a hearty chuckle. Whatcha afraid of? Snakes? Lions? Spiders? Why, there is nothing in this here jungle that this little beauty can't take care of." He patted his pistol. "She is sighted in and ready to go."

Dix turned to Hardy and pointed a finger. "You best make sure you aren't shooting at us when we go to relieve ourselves." Dixon stretched out on the ground and placed his high-crowned, wide-brimmed, sable fedora over his face before I could get a look at his face.

Hardy scratched at his stubbly beard. "Maybe we should have a signal if someone has to go."

"I will be sure to tell you, Hardy." Dix said and rolled away from his company.

The fire dimmed with the passing hours. Everyone was asleep. Even the man they referred to as Hardy McBride, who was supposed to be keeping watch, is sleeping soundly. He may have been able to stay awake if he did not continue to consume the alcohol until he passed out. It was the break that I needed.

I shimmied down the backside of the tree, under the cloak of darkness, and plotted my path to Olivia. It had to be done in one quick movement so that I didn't wake the others.

Before I moved forward, I counted the people sleeping in the circle. Alice had Olivia on one side of her and the man she calls Dix on the other side. Across from her was the drunkard, Hardy McBride, with a hefty Griffin Stone next to him. The snoring was a good sign that I can get to Olivia. Still, I had to be quick.

I heard a rustling sound behind me that made the hair on the back of my neck stand on end. There is little illumination from the moon in the dense trees and I was blind to the dangers behind me. I could only see what was close to the fire's dimming light and what reflected off the fire's flames.

Low to the ground, a single pair of glowing eyes peered in my direction. As it approached with its beady eyes finding prey, in a split second, the small lizard was devoured. The civet is a funny creature and harmless to me. It has a unique coat of black and white stripes and splotches that cover his fur. He wore a black furry mask around his eyes that made him look mischievous.

I quietly lifted Olivia, Jeena, and the blanket from the ground and stepped back into the trees. The darkness encompassed any trace of us. We vanished from the fire and I began to move blindly in the dark.

When we were far enough away from the men, I untied Olivia's arms and removed the gag. She rubbed at her arms where the rope chaffed her skin. "Mommy, I knew you would come for me. I knew you would find me. I tried to be brave. Was I brave, Mommy?"

I grabbed Olivia's hand as I walked through the jungle with the only light to guide us being the moonlight that occasionally peaked through the trees. I was walking out of memory. "You were very brave. There isn't a braver child on the earth," I whispered.

"I learned from you."

I stopped. "What? Why from me?"

"You are Jane, Mommy. Jane knew how to beat the men in the jungle. Jane climbed the cliff and hid Tim in the cave. She was very brave. I knew that you could do it again. I waited for you, but I was still scared of the man. He is Dixon, but Alice calls him Dix."

It was the reminder that I needed. I only focused on the bad that had happened. The situation. I forgot to focus on how I had survived using my skills in the wild. Olivia always wanted to hear the story because she knew it was about me and my life in the jungle. She saw the story as her mother conquering the world, while I saw it as a tragedy.

"Yes, Olivia, I am Jane from the story. I won't let anyone harm you. We are going to get out of here. We just need to climb to the top of the trees. Remember the silly monkeys in the story? Do you remember how they went to the tops of the trees to escape danger? We don't want to be like Jabari. He climbed down and pestered the leopard. We want to be like the rest of the monkeys. I am going to need you to climb."

"I can't climb, Mommy." Worriment covered her dirty face. "I don't know how and it's too dark to see my hands and feet."

"Don't worry, Olivia. I will help you, just start looking for the next branch, feel for it. Make it one that is close to you and feels thick so that it holds your weight. Watch where you put your feet. I will be right behind you, so don't worry."

The monkeys knew of our presence. They sat watching us from their perches above us. I can only make out their outline, but they are unmistakably monkeys. It's their smell that offends my senses.

It's true that I learned how to climb by watching them as a child. As an adult, I don't really care for them. Their shadowy figures nervously stir and pace. But it is not only our presence that is making them nervous. There is something else hunting in the night.

Silence eerily hung in the air as the monkeys stopped their sounds and movements. A low growl echoed in the stillness.

Nothing moved. The animals know, as I know, that there is danger in the jungle. Some animals remain silent to hide from the danger. Some animals are silent and *are* dangerous.

The smell of death hangs in the air'. It is close enough to touch. The smell of blood that draws in every keen nose.

"Come here," Olivia," I said, positioning myself on a large tree branch big enough to cradle me in its limbs. I held Olivia and she yawned. She turned to look at me with her exhausted, droopy eyes.

Her long lashes fluttered and her eyes closed. "You let them take me. What if you let them take me again?"

It felt like a slap. "Olivia, I didn't let them take you."

"Yes, you did." Olivia began to whimper. "I was scared when they took me. You were supposed to protect me."

Wasn't this conversation similar to the discussion I had recently with my own mother? Didn't I blame her for not protecting me? Now I know how hurt Momma must have felt when I blamed her for the horrors of my childhood. It was the same conversation coming back to haunt me. I made a mental note to tell my mother how much I love her when I return home. I will make sure that our bond is impenetrable.

I began to rock her in my arms. "I'm sorry, Olivia. I didn't know they took you until I found the note and I got here just as soon as I could."

"What about Charlie? Did you leave him to get poached again?"

"Charlie was not poached. He just had blood on himself from the elephant."

"But you didn't stop the bad people from killing the baby elephant, right Mommy?" Olivia rubbed at her sleepy eyes.

"Why don't we rest? I will hold you and you can hold Jeena."

"I'm sleepy," she said with a yawn.

"I know you are. Let's just rest here." I adjusted my position to be as comfortable as possible. Olivia fell into a peaceful slumber within minutes.

We were cradled in nature's arms, high above the jungle floor and away from dangers, both animal and human.

It wasn't long before sunrise and the jungle began to stir. We were awakened with the echoes of the birds' songs that mingled with the sounds of the cicada; that long, repeated piercing sound.

The deep wailing noise of the hippo's aggression in the distance, and the screech of a troop of howler monkeys communicating was upsetting Olivia. "Mommy, I don't like when the animals yell like that; I think they are mad at us for being in their home. Don't they know that we live here too?"

"No, they are not mad. They are just telling each other that we are here. That's all. There is nothing to worry about. Do you remember in my story about Jane, when she swung in the trees? When I swung in the trees?" I corrected my statement.

"Yes."

"The monkeys were my friends. I learned to climb and swing by watching them."

"Is that true?" Olivia asked.

"Of course it's true."

"Then maybe I can watch Jeena and she can teach me."

"I don't want you to climb in the trees after we get home. It is too dangerous."

"But you did it," Olivia challenged.

"I was older. And I didn't have parents to watch my every move. They both worked a lot. You do."

"It's not fair."

"Olivia, life is not fair. So you have to learn to do what you are told. Now, we are going to have to climb higher into the trees. We are safer in the trees than on the ground. If we look out for the snakes and monkeys, we are much safer. So, we will stay in the trees as long as we can and go down when we have to."

A snap of a limb caught my attention and my hand flew to my mouth to motion for Olivia to be still and silent. I heard the crack of branches again. A nearby tree was uprooted by the troop of gorillas moving into the territory. A large male, with his broad chest and huge head was trying to show off his strength for the females in the troop. He snapped the tiny trees and sent them crashing to the ground. His silver back gave away his adulthood, along with his 300-pound stature. Beautiful, but fierce, his black fur covered most of his body. His eyes were the color of a moonless night. He is dark and very dangerous.

Another male gorilla's stance boasted a challenge to the huge male. The challenger was smaller, maybe younger and too pushy to go unnoticed by the dominant male.

They showed their enormous teeth at each other to establish dominance as they faced off. The larger male grabbed the other and shoved him into the tree that housed us, causing the tree to shake.

Olivia let out a scream and grabbed tightly to me. She covered her mouth with her hand but it was too late.

I pulled her tightly against me and she buried her head into me. In my mind, I knew that we were in a very bad place, so I thought quickly. Somehow, I must draw their attention away from us. From Olivia.

That's when I noticed the silence on the ground beneath us. In fact, there were no other sounds around us. The birds were silently waiting to take flight to avoid being a part of the trouble. The little monkeys had taken off to the safety high above in the canopy. There was silence in the trees and the only sound I heard was my own quickly beating heart.

The gorillas tried to locate the direction of the scream. With several grunts from the large male gorilla, the group huddled together in a defensive stance, careful not to show their backs to the dense jungle. Their circle of unity was terrifying.

"Be still," I whispered in Olivia's ear. "Be very still."

We are careful to be motionless and silent.

The largest male sniffed at the air and followed the scent to our tree. His dark eyes locked on our location and he let out a wail that vibrated in my chest. Olivia cried and covered her ears.

"Move!" I yelled and started to push Olivia higher into the tree. "Olivia, climb like Jabari! Climb faster! Don't stop until you are with the little monkeys high up in the trees!"

She grabbed for the next limb and pulled herself up. "Mommy. I can't move too fast."

"Just climb. Don't look back. Get high enough that the limbs are very small. He can't get you on the small limbs, He is too big."

"Alright," Olivia whimpered and continued to climb.

The large male shook the tree vigorously, trying to knock us off a limb, but we were too far up for his attempt to matter.

He began to climb. The gorilla is frighteningly fast. Faster than I could ever climb.

The only thing I can focus on is Olivia. She has to get up higher.

"Keep going. I will be right there," I yelled to Olivia, who continued to slowly make her way up into the leaves.

Olivia looked back at me. Her frightened face gave way to tears and she pleaded with me. "Mommy, don't leave me. I'm scared."

"Be brave, Olivia, and get Jeena and yourself to safety."

I swung to an adjourning tree, calling for the gorilla to follow me. "Hey! Over here! Come and get me!" My yelling worked and he was now focused in my direction. He swung effortlessly to another tree, and then another. My abilities came back to me and my pace quickened. I fearlessly grabbed and swung to keep moving further from Olivia and he followed.

He was fast and had a look of fury on his face. His brow was furrowed, his eyes focused and his mouth open, revealing his enormous white teeth.

I was not faster than him, and before I could get high enough, he was closing in on me. I decided that I would make my stand against him on the very limb that I was standing on. I grabbed my sack and struggled with the closure. My shaking hands prevented me from being quick enough, and he was only a few swings from getting to me. As I reached in my bag for my gun and pulled it out, the Silver Back landed on the limb. He caused a tremble in the limb and I dropped my gun. It landed with a thud on the jungle floor.

The gorilla stood upright, showing his tall stature. His mobility was my curse.

I backed up as far as I could go, my back to the tree.

He raised his arms, beat on his chest to show his dominance and he screamed a terrifying scream.

I know to lower my gaze. Direct eye contact would be interpreted as a challenge, which I clearly do not intend to do.

The Silverback was barely a foot away from me. He pounded on the tree next to my head and screamed so loud in my face, that I wanted to be sick or pass out from fear. I felt the force of his breath on my face. He let out another angry yell just inches from me. I didn't dare move. I remained submissive and still.

Suddenly a shot rang out and the troop of gorillas scattered into the underbrush. One gorilla lay at the bottom of the tree, struggling to get up.

Before the Silverback climbed away from me, he gave me one more terrorizing snarl.

I quickly swung away and climbed to Olivia. She visibly relaxed when I reached her. I placed my hand over Olivia's mouth. "Close your eyes Olivia and be silent."

She nodded her head and flinched when another shot rang out, taking the wounded gorilla's life. Only one predator carries a gun.

I noticed Alice pacing, with her hands covering her ears. "Did you really have to shoot that monkey, Dix? Did ya?"

"It's a gorilla and yes, I had to kill it before it killed any of us. Don't you see the size of that thing? Why, it would eat you as soon as look at you."

Griffin Stone waddled over to the dead gorilla and kicked its foot with his boot. "Looks dead alright. Whatcha say we get some grub before we move on. Killings always make me hungry," he chuckled."

Dix begins to pace below our hiding place in the tree. "Everything makes you hungry. I swear, if you didn't have those muscles, you'd be fat. We can't stop. No, we have to find them. And when I do, it will be sweet revenge. Finally, his death will not be in vain."

Alice shakes her head. "You know you really should try to get over this hatred and move on with your life. Maybe we get married and settle down somewhere warm. Like Florida or somethin'," Alice said.

"You don't understand. You had both of your parents. I didn't. After my pop never came back from doing this job in the jungle, I have had to deal with the hurt on my mother's face when she worked her fingers to the bone trying to put food on our table. She worked hard, God rest her soul."

Dix looked skyward as he reminisced on his dead mother. And that's when I saw it. I should have pieced it together earlier. That tall build. Dark and dangerous features, that voice. My hand was no longer on Olivia's mouth, but on my own. Oh, how I wanted to scream but I couldn't risk giving away our location. I knew that man who only now lived in my nightmares. The man below was a spitting image of him. Of course he is. He happens to be his son. The man below me was the son of Bain.

Bain who hunted me in the jungle. Who shot me at Thinking Rock. Bain who screamed the name Jane with that crazed look on his face and angered Tembo. That will always haunt me. He called me Jane until his dying breath and Tembo had killed him quickly by piercing him with his tusk and trampling him with his large foot.

I was right back in my nightmare. Right back where it all began. I was being chased again by Bain.

CHAPTER 7

Dixon moved on with Alice walking closely behind him. Hardy and Griffin cleared a path before them. They were not experienced enough to see the trail made by the animals.

"They must be headed back to the house, to the elephant farm. If we move fast, we can catch them. We're not stopping for the night this time."

Olivia wrapped her arms around my neck. She could barely keep her eyes open. "I needed something to drink and a nap. That scary gorilla made me so afraid that I was suddenly tired. Do we have food?" Olivia asked.

"Yes, we have food."

"I'm sorry, Mommy. I can't climb any longer. Can we please get down?"

"Yes, let's go down and rest."

We slowly climbed down.

I scouted the area using all of my senses. I don't see any immediate danger. There were no sounds to indicate trouble in the area and there was no foul smell in the air.

Olivia, with Jeena on her shoulder, walked over to the dead gorilla. She stroked his fur. "Why do they do that? Why are they always killing the animals? He didn't have to die. He wasn't the one that was going to hurt us."

"I know, Olivia. I can't answer the question as to why people kill. They just do. It's sad, I know. But we cannot stay here. Another animal will smell the blood in the air and we don't want to be here when they come."

We rested and ate some of the provisions that I brought with me. Olivia was unusually quiet. The entire event has been too much for her, so I did what any mother would do. I leaned against a tree, well hidden from view and I held her close and rocked her, singing a lullaby in her ear. It wasn't long before she fell asleep. A little rest will do her good. And it would give me time to think.

We were so far from home, and Alice and the men will naturally think we would go in that direction. There is no easy way to get there. Either we travel in the same direction as Dixon Bain and his crew, or we go around toward Thinking Rock where we have a better chance of hiding. I chose Thinking Rock.

If I can get us to the waterfall, we can hide in the cave. But I needed to get home before they got there to warn Izzy and Momma. I knew if they'd lost Olivia, they might take Charlie or worse. Either way, they'd wait for me to get there. I needed a plan.

Olivia woke from her slumber and she didn't seem as scared as she was earlier.

We hadn't gotten far and I smelled smoke and noticed trouble ahead of us. I saw the smoldering signs of a fire. From the look of the ground and the way they left some of their gear, I would say that they left in a hurry.

The footprints left by gorillas showed that the gorillas were chasing Bain and his crew.

"Olivia, we have to go another way. It's not safe to travel in this direction."

She nodded and followed me through an unfamiliar part of the jungle. I had no way of knowing whether I was back on Swavendi land or the other tribe's land. "Stay really close and keep quiet," I whispered to Olivia.

"Do you know where we are going?"

No, I do not, but we have to get away from the bad people and the gorillas."

"I don't like the gorillas. I don't like those people either."

"Me either."

I carried my barefoot child, who was still dressed for sleep on my back for a long distance for two reasons. I didn't want her to get stuck by a thorn or worse, and if someone were tracking, they would only see one set of footprints. I cautiously and slowly walked through the dense, undisturbed trees. There was no chance of sunlight getting through the thick foliage. Strange new plants were everywhere and blocking my path. I had no way of knowing whether they were helpful or dangerous. "Don't touch anything. We don't know these plants."

"I won't," Olivia answered.

The undergrowth was thick. Large spike-like thorns protruded from the unknown plants and I felt the sharp slice on my skin. I looked down to find a lengthy gash on the side of my lower leg. "Crap." I stopped to assess the damage.

I placed Olivia on a small clearing.

Olivia noticed the blood running from the wound. "Mommy. You are hurt."

"I'm alright."

"You are bleeding. That isn't alright." She pointed at my bleeding leg. Whatever was on that needle, or spear-like plant caused a deep burning in my wound. I opened the canteen and poured water on it to dilute and rinse out the toxin or whatever was causing the burning pain.

"Mommy, the blood is still coming out." Olivia looked worriedly at the laceration.

"You are right, it is bleeding, but I know what to do."

"What will you do?" Olivia asked excitedly.

"I want you to watch me carefully."

I searched until I found the driver ants. I looked for the large soldier ants. Carefully, I picked them up and put their powerful jaws on both sides of the gash. I squeezed the skin together and when they bit down they clenched on both sides of the deep cut. When the ants were secured, I broke off the rest of their body, leaving them attached as a sort of stitch to hold the wound together.

My father told me about that trick when I was little. I never thought I would have to use it. I was grateful to know it.

Olivia's face was close to my leg. She watched the process over and over, with each ant, until the wound was shut. "Doesn't that hurt when they bite you?" Olivia asked.

"It does hurt, but I know that it will help me until I can get home and stitch it up correctly. Grandpa is a very smart man and he told me how to do this when I was young."

"Can we try it on Charlie the next time when he gets hurt?"

"No. We are not trying this on Charlie. This is only used in an emergency when there is no other way, like now."

"I miss my brother," Olivia pouted.

"I miss him too."

"And I miss Daddy, and Grandpa, and Uncle Tim too. When will they be home? When can I see them again?"

"Soon. We will see them all soon." I answered, hoping it was the truth.

The hours passed. We were away from the strange plants and continued to move forward.

Olivia was enjoying the feel of the fallen leaves on her bare feet. She called it squishy.

She danced around, unaware of what might be in front of us. The wildness of it all had taken her over and she became more daring with each step.

Suddenly, I froze. There was a large ravine in our path and grabbed Olivia before she tumbled into it. There were plenty of trees and vines on this side of the gorge and plenty on the other side, vines I could use to get across the wide distance, but I knew I couldn't do it with Olivia on my back. And I also knew she could not do it on her own.

I began to estimate different distances, looking for a narrower gap to carry her across with me. The options looked bleak.

It seemed as though the ravine was long enough to split the jungle in half.

I calculated the jump again in my mind. The length of the perfect swinging vine, the speed with which I would need to swing to make it safely across, and the width of the ravine with its sharp rocky bottom.

Mid-thought and out of the corner of my eye, I saw Olivia's movement. She ran as fast as she could, grabbed a random vine and swung out over the ravine.

I tried to reach for her, but it was too late. She was midair and halfway over the ravine. I watched in horror as she confidently swung her feet higher to gain an extra lift and she gracefully landed on the other side. "Come on Mommy! Don't we have to go?"

I was speechless. My mind was struggling to grasp what had just happened. "But how?"

"I just did it."

There I was calculating distances, lengths and looking for a narrowing in the distance, while Olivia just grabbed a vine and fearlessly jumped.

She has a natural ability that I have been ignoring. She is not a strong climber, but, man, can she swing.

"Aren't you coming Mommy?" She called to me.

I matched her whimsical and daring move. I grabbed the nearest vine and propelled myself across with ease.

"You surprise me, Olivia."

"Why? Didn't you think I could do it?"

"Honestly, no. I didn't think that you could swing so good."

"You should have, Mommy."

"Really? Why should I have known that you could swing like that?"

"Because I am your daughter. Doesn't that mean that I can also be brave and do stuff like that in the jungle?"

"Stuff like that, huh. Yes, I suppose that you could."

"No, I can." Olivia stamped her foot.

"Okay, okay. You can."

"She grinned and turned to walk in front of me on the path. "Not so fast, young lady. One jump does not mean you know what you are doing in the jungle."

I moved in front of Olivia and kept a steady pace.

It was late afternoon before I heard the rushing sounds of the water spilling over the cliffs. "We are close, Olivia. Just a little more to go and we will be at the waterfall. You know what that means from the stories, right?"

"The hidden cave! The one that you and Uncle Tim used to get away from the bad man."

"That's right. The cave. We need shelter for the night. Home is just too far to make it home before night comes. It will be dark, but nobody else knows about it, so we can be sure to be safe.

The great pool of water at the bottom of the waterfall was my swimming hole as a child. Tembo and I spent a lot of time floating in these waters. Oh, how I missed my brave Tembo. There was no chance that he would come and save me this time. His death by poachers would forever be an empty hole in my heart.

We traveled to the water and followed it to the bottom of the rocks on the side of the waterfall.

I looked up to see Thinking Rock. I could climb it blindfolded. Olivia cannot.

I probably shouldn't doubt her abilities as much. She showed me that she has those swinging talents, but I know her not to be a climber.

I had just visited the cave not too long ago and I remembered what I had left there. My father's knife. I never stopped to find my gun when the gorilla made me drop it from the tree. I should have.

With the gun gone, it would be a great advantage to have the extra knife. I was not afraid to use it on whomever I had to, to keep us safe and protect my child.

We reached the bottom of the cliff that led to the cave. Olivia looked frightened at the rushing water. "Mommy, I can't go in there. It's too fast."

"We are not going in the water, there is a secret cave. It's hidden. See the side of the cliff over there?"

"Yes."

"We are going to climb up the rocks. It will be like going up the steps at home, just slippery."

"Ok. I can do it."

I patted her head and grabbed her hand. "Let's make it our own adventure."

I knew that keeping the mood light would help her to focus on something other than falling.

"What if I fall?"

So now I see that it's too late for games. Olivia was already worried, not that I blamed her.

I said the first thing that came to mind. "Then you can swim. I know you like to do that. And I will jump in too and we will swim home."

"I'm a good swimmer, Mommy. Faster than Daddy sometimes. He even says he doesn't let me win."

"You are a great swimmer, Olivia. But let's try not to fall in, okay?"

"Okay."

We slowly scaled the slippery, cool rocks. Twice, I thought I would lose Olivia when she began to slide toward the edge. I was vigilant enough to keep a hold of her arm and pull her back to the semi-safety of the rock wall.

The cave opened in front of us. Once inside, I turned on my flashlight so that I could see to light a fire. Luckily the wood I'd placed here before was still stacked and dry.

I found my father's knife and secured it in my boot for safe keeping.

"What's this?" Olivia was holding my old doll, the one that I'd left on the woodpile.

"That is my doll. I left it here when I was a little girl and thought that I was too old to play with her anymore."

"Can I keep it?"

"Of course, you can keep the doll. I've wanted you to have it when we came up here, I just never told you about it."

Olivia's face shone. Her smile told me that she may indeed be strong enough to forget these events. She's younger than I was when I was tortured. Maybe all of this will be forgotten.

Olivia held the doll to her chest and stroked Jeena's tail with her other hand. "Jeena is getting bigger and she doesn't like to be wrapped in my blanket anymore. I can use this baby doll instead. Would that be alright?"

I smiled at Olivia's excited face. "Yes, you may keep the doll and wrap her in a million blankets if you want."

She sat down on the dirty cave floor near the fire and carefully folded the blanket around the doll. Jeena sat on Olivia's shoulder to observe the tedious process.

A distraction from our situation is exactly what Olivia needed.

The day's journey that turned into night left me utterly exhausted, but I knew we would be safe in the cave and I would be able to get some much needed sleep. I kept an eye on my leg wound. My body needed to rest and recover.

I placed more wood on the fire and cuddled up next to Olivia. The fire would protect us from predators and an onslaught of bugs.

Olivia snuggled in close to me and hugged the doll instead of her monkey.

I breathed deeply to take in the scent of her. She smelled of earth, with a hint of monkey. It's not the best smell, but somehow it was comforting to my soul.

Jeena curled her body around Olivia's head and we all fell asleep.

I was awakened from my restless slumber by a hard tapping on my boot.

Dixon Bain!

He was standing over me, pointing a rifle at my rapidly beating heart.

Olivia's head lay on my chest. If he were to shoot, both Olivia and I would be dead.

"Wake up," he snarled. "Wow! Look how peaceful she sleeps." Dixon's words dripped with sarcasm. "Pretty soon, you will be sleeping for a long time. A very long time. An eternity; you *and* your kid."

Instinctually, I lay a protective hand on Olivia's head. "Olivia, wake up. You have to wake up."

Olivia saw Dixon and screamed. "No, I am not going with you again! Leave us alone!"

Dixon's face reddened. "Shut your kid up or she will be the first to go. Actually, that's not a bad idea. You can watch while I put a bullet in her head."

Griffin stood behind Dixon with another rifle poised to shoot. He was a foot taller than Dixon, so I could see his face clearly. He had a look as though he had eaten something extremely sour. His eyes were squinty, his lips were curled into a snarl. I believed that he could be a murderer, a torturer, a man without feelings or regret.

I quickly stood and placed Olivia behind me. "You will not hurt my child." I hissed.

It only made Dixon laugh. "You are in no position to snarl at me. You had this coming!"

"You can't hold me responsible for your father's actions. That's insane. He hunted me like a wild animal!"

My composure slipped over the edge, teetering toward hysteria. My heart was beating wildly and my breath quickened as my mind raced, looking for a way out. All the muscles in my body tensed and I wanted to lunge at Dixon, but I knew I didn't stand a chance against two men with rifles. I couldn't outrun a bullet. And there was Olivia.

Dixon was already there. His mind was broken. He drew closer, only inches from my face. "My father ran into you and he never came home. The reports said that he was trampled by an elephant. Your elephant!" Dixon's eyes radiated contempt. His face was so close to mine that his spittle sprayed my face.

I countered his contempt. "Tembo was protecting me!"

"And you celebrated the animal that murdered my father. Isn't that what all the fuss is about? You start the Tembo Project to rejoice in the animal that you used to kill my father!"

"That's not it. Tembo was poached. He was killed by men who carved him up for his tusks." A single tear made its way down my cheek. The memory stung worse than a a swarm of yellow jacket bees.

A laugh escaped Dixon's lips. "Are we going to cry about it?" he taunted. "If he was still alive, I would have already slaughtered him and made you bathe in his blood!" Dixon scowled.

Alice had just made it over the top of the ridge to the cave. Her pants and her blouse were torn, her hair disheveled and she had a murderous look on her face. She cleared her throat and moved toward Dixon; her hands clenched at her side.

"Dix, you left me on that slippery ledge all by myself! I could have broken my neck. Just because you and your hired gorilla here are good climbers, doesn't mean I am. Do you ever think about anyone but yourself? Do you, Dixon Bain?" she said, grabbing his arm.

Dixon nudged Alice away. "You've done your job, Alice. I just needed you around to take care of the kid. You are of no use to me now. So, shut your mouth or you can join her and the kid!"

His words wounded Alice's feelings and the tears slipped down her face.

Dixon turned his attention back to me. "I was only a kid when he died. He never came home. Do you remember Lonnie? Of course you do. He was the only man that you didn't get killed. Lonnie visited me after his return trip with Tim and he told me all about the brave little girl that survived the men and saved her precious Tim by hiding him in the cave by the towering cliff. How hard do you think it was to find you when the cliff sticks out like a sore thumb? Also, you have not been keeping the kid quiet. Her voice was easy to track. You repeated the same mistake. You thought this place would keep you safe." Dixon's voice trailed off.

"Correction, I didn't get them killed. That was their own doing." I stated.

"You killed them just as sure as if you'd stuck the knife in them with your own hands! Everyone but Lonnie. Well, him and Tim. Lonnie tried to convince me that my father was a bad person. He said that my father tried to kill you and the boy. So, as you can see, you survived and my father didn't. You are the reason he never came home!"

"I am not responsible for what your father did. He did try to kill me and my brother."

"Ah, yes, Tim became your brother. That boy that got in the way of Warren? Do I have that right? His uncle wanted him dead, not my father. My father was a protector of Warren."

"Your father was the one who was going to kill us, not Warren. Your father was a crazed murderer!" I picked up Olivia to ensure that I could move with her. I circled the fire. With the water to my back and the fire in front, I was surrounded by opposites. Just like Dixon and me. I try to save lives and he tries to take them.

I could feel the spray of water from the waterfall at my back and took a small step toward the ledge.

Dixon countered my move and drew closer. "Stop moving!" he yelled.

I took smaller steps backward and disguised the movements as adjusting Olivia on my hip. "Your father was a mean and hateful person. He even killed one of the men in their group."

I inched closer and closer to the edge of the waterfall. There was nowhere else to go.

Distracting Dixon by talking could buy me enough time to think of a plan. "Looks like you are missing one of your men. What happened, did the gorillas get him? He was not equipped to be in this jungle. What was his name, Hardy McBride, right?"

Alice hid behind Dixon, looking more disheveled than she would care to know. Her makeup ran below her eyes, the whiteness of her clothing gave way to the earthy jungles brown and green colors. Her hair looked like it had a mind of its own, standing on end in a nest of unkempt curls.

Alice shook with anxiety. "They ate Hardy's face! That's what they did! Those stupid monkeys chased us, and he was too slow on account of his size and all. He was too heavy to be light on his feet. They ate him!" She was bordering on madness.

"They are gorillas. Yes, I saw what they did to him. That's what they do. If you make eye contact or show any aggression, they will kill you. But you wouldn't know that, would you? You are lucky that they didn't do the same to you. None of you belongs in this jungle. You are not prepared to be here," I said.

Alice was delirious now, shaking her head. "She's right, Dix. We don't belong here. It's too much. Maybe we should just go home!"

"The only person going anywhere is her," he said, raising the gun to point at my head. She is going to the grave!" Dixon shoved the gun a little closer to my face.

Jeena screeched and climbed to Olivia's shoulder. Olivia held tightly to me. "Make him stop, Mommy," she cried. "Jeena doesn't like him. I don't either."

Dixon sneered at me with his evil smile. "Taking orders from a monkey, are we?"

I figured that if I could get Alice on my side, maybe I would be able to use her as a distraction. "Alice, is this really who you are?

A kidnapper of an innocent child? A murderer? I've watched you with Olivia. You were kind to my daughter. I won't forget that."

Alice ran her hands through her curls, trying to calm them. "Oh, um, she's just a kid. Dix said that she wouldn't be hurt." Her eyes nervously darted from me to the fire.

"You believe that?"

Alice stepped forward and looked from me to Dixon and back to me. "Um, I have to believe that he will change his mind about this whole thing and we can all go home."

Dixon grabbed Alice by the arm and shoved her backward. "That's enough talking. You knew the plan from the very beginning. There will be no changing my mind. Jane has to die."

"It's Zura! My name is not Jane!" I screamed.

In the three seconds Dixon was distracted by pushing Alice, he had turned slightly away from me. Still holding Olivia, I grabbed my father's knife from my boot and lunged quickly toward Dixon. I held the knife to Dixon's throat, pushing gently to maintain my leverage. A small amount of blood escaped from his skin. His eyes widened in shock. Every part of me wanted to slice his throat. Just a clean line to end the torment. I don't believe it would be murder if I was saving our lives.

I squeezed the knife, adding to the pressure of the cut. I moved my hand and the weight of guilt stopped me from continuing to cut. His hand flew up to grab the knife. With the sight of his blood against the metal blade, I knew that this would be my only chance to kill him and my determination was failing.

Within seconds, I heard the clicking of a gun and saw Griffin from the corner of my eye. He raised his pistol to my head, and I lowered the knife.

Dixon's hand reached in his pants pocket and he retrieved a handkerchief. He applies pressure to the wound. "Well, now you have done it. A simple flesh wound. That's all you are capable of, right? You don't have the guts to kill me even when you have the chance. You are weak," he said and picked up his rifle.

"You don't have to do this, Dixon."

"Oh, I know I don't have to, Jungle Girl. But I want to. Now more than ever!"

I feigned surrender and raised my free hand, pretending to give in as I began to step in front of Dixon, toward the sheet the waterfall.

"What are you going to do? Jump and kill you and your child? I don't think so. You are not that stupid."

That's exactly what I was thinking, only I know where the rocks are you ignorant baboon. I ignored his words and took another step backward.

Dixon began to laugh. "Look at you! Always defiant. You never give up, do you?"

I took another step. "Never."

"I'll shoot you right through your child, Jane."

I take my last step backward. The tumbling water's deafening crash drowned out all other sounds. "I am Zura. My name is Zura, not Jane!"

Olivia brought her little lips to my ear. "You are Jane," Olivia said. "You are Jane and that means nobody can hurt you."

I am always amazed at how Olivia sees me. Her message was the reminder that I needed.

I stared into the eyes of my brave girl. They were the color of the trees and the jungle grass. Brown, green, with a hint of yellow. There is nothing guarded in those bright eyes. I am Jane. Not the scared Jane that faced the evil when I was a little girl. I am the gown woman Jane who protects her family. The Jane that Olivia saw in me. I am Jane.

I felt the fear and anger bubbling from my stomach. It traveled up to my throat until I could no longer push it down. Hot tears streamed from my eyes. Olivia was so innocent to the ways of the world.

"Let's go home, Mommy," Olivia said. "Do it, Mommy. I'm a good swimmer, remember?"

I knew that we had a better chance of surviving the water than we did with Dixon's maniacal quest for revenge. I knew that I probably should jump. *Get as far away from Dixon Bain as you can get. But if I jump, I may kill Olivia. What if I live and she dies? I would never forgive myself. And what if I die and she lives? How will she find her way home? She would be prey to every wild cat in the jungle.*

The only thing I knew for sure was that if I didn't jump, Dixon would kill both of us.

As Dixon readjusted his gun to shoot, Alice grabbed his arm to stop him. "No!" Alice screamed.

A bullet pinged off the cave wall and I moved.

I held Olivia tightly. "Remember to hold your breath," I whispered to Olivia.

I leaped into rushing water. As we floated effortlessly on the misty air, we simultaneously wrapped ourselves around each other. Olivia held on tight to Jeena, tucking her body into mine. I prayed we would not hit the rocks below.

Within seconds that felt like forever, we hit the water. It took my breath away and I lost my grip on Olivia. The impact sent me spiraling toward the rocky bed beneath the water's surface. I rode the rushing water toward its depths, kicking wildly to slow my descent.

"Olivia!" I screamed as I resurfaced. There was no sign of her. "Olivia!" A torturous wail escaped my lips.

I dove swiftly. Fully submerged in the turbulent water, I looked for her. I was surrounded by the continuous rushing of water. Then I saw her and I was compelled to stop and watch. There was no panic; no fear guided her motions. She moved gracefully, like a bird soaring in the air. Her hands and feet glided simultaneously as she rose to the surface. I followed her to the top and swam to her.

Crashing white torrents whirled us in their quake, but they did not frighten her.

Olivia's smiling face greeted me as she shook water from her face. She is treading water, unaware of the rocks or the dangers that might have been lurking below us. "I told you I was a good swimmer," she beamed.

"You are an excellent swimmer." I wanted to cry with joy.

"That was fun!" she smiled with those dimples. "Can we do that again sometime, Mommy?"

I just smiled. She even managed to hold on to my old rag doll.

The sound of gunshots and the splashing of bullets hitting the water now had my attention. "We have to move, Olivia. Can you swim under the water? Swim to the side. See the trees? There is a good cover in the trees."

A scream interrupted our focus. I looked up to see a screaming and flailing Alice plummeting toward the water. She hit the water hard.

I looked at Olivia and pointed to the banks. "Swim to the biggest tree and get behind it. Hurry!"

I dove under the frothy water to find Alice. She was sinking quickly. The panic on her face and the scream that escaped her lips sent the rest of the air in her lungs into the water. Air bubbles escaped her and floated toward the top.

I quickly swam to her and grabbed her by the arm to tow her to the surface.

Even as we reached the surface, she gasped for air and her limbs went stiff in a panic.

She flailed her arms in terror. She sputtered water, trying to speak. "I can't swim! I can't swim!" Her words came in gasps, but the message was clear.

Alice smacked me in the face with her thrashing arm.

"Stop moving!" I yelled. "I'm trying to help you."

Suddenly her body went limp and she passed out from terror.

I preferred her unconscious.

I swam to the bank and hauled Alice up with me. She was coming to when I dragged her body onto the bank. I strained to get her behind the tree. "We can't stay here. Dixon will be coming down the cliff as fast as he can."

Alice was mumbling and holding her head. "I'm going to drown. My shoes, I don't have my shoes."

"We don't have time for this. We have to get moving!"

Olivia was crying.

"Olivia, are you hurt? What's wrong?" I asked.

"Jeena!" Olivia wailed. "Where is my baby monkey? I don't know where she is. Can you help me find her?"

"Olivia, Jeena will be alright. She's a quick little monkey and can outrun and outmaneuver those men. But we won't be if we don't get moving. We have to go. I promise that after this is over, we will find your monkey or she will find us. But right now, we have to go."

Olivia sniffed back the rest of her tears and silently nodded in agreement.

Alice pulled on my arm to get my attention. I looked at her vulnerable eyes and tousled appearance. Her white outfit is mud-covered and torn. Wet black hair hung in her eyes like a curled black mamba.

Gone was the perfectly coiffed shiny mane. Her makeup was washed away except for the black streaks that ran down her face from her eyes.. The true Alice before me, broken and disheveled. "What about my shoes? I can't go trampling through this jungle without shoes! I'm not barbaric," Alice cried.

"You sure look the part right now," I answered. "Isn't that how you treated my daughter? Didn't you snatch her without shoes to walk through this jungle? But hey, if you want to hang around and look for your shoes, be my guest. I'm taking Olivia and getting out of here. You're welcome to come with us."

With down-cast eyes, she took a moment to consider my words. Her hands fly up to her hair. "Oh, this was a big mistake. This whole trip is killing me. Look at me! I'm a mess. I can't find my way out of here. You have to help me!" Alice stood and grabbed my arms.

"I don't have to do anything. I saved you out of human decency. But do not confuse my help with giving you any more than you gave to Olivia," I said. "Let's go."

Traveling became difficult. Alice was slow and irritating. She continuously stopped to complain about something digging into her feet. Being barefoot was punishing on those pampered feet.

And because of this slow pace, we are losing the head start we had over Dixon and Griffin.

My feet were toughened for this environment. Alice's were not. I quickly sat down and untied my boots. "I don't know what size you are, and I don't really care. Put these on," I said tossing my boots at Alice's feet.

"You are giving me your boots?" Alice questioned as though I had just handed her a fistful of diamonds.

"I guess so," I said with a shrug. "We have to get moving or he will catch up to us."

"I'm much obliged," Alice smiled slightly. She put on my boots.

I lifted Olivia onto my back and we began to increase our pace toward my home.

Alice shuffled her feet when she walked, making an unwelcoming sound. "Do you have to do that? You are drawing too much attention to us."

"These boots are a little too big, but I'm grateful. You know, I bet everything you own would be too big on me." Alice continued to shuffle her feet.

I sighed loudly enough for her to hear my frustration. "If you are trying to insult me, you are doing a lousy job."

"Oh no, Zura, you misunderstand me. I only meant that you are tall and thin and beautiful. I am short. Why, you would be a famous model in the United States. Agents would be crawling all over you to sign with them. You could be very rich."

"Money doesn't hold the same appeal to me as it does to others. I've never had it. I don't need it here."

"What about fame?" You don't understand the buzz that's happening in Chicago, in New York. All over the States. Everyone wants to meet the real Jungle Girl that took down the poachers with little more than her keen sense of the jungle. Don't be surprised when visitors start showing up. They'll come to see you. Although, it may anger you to know that they call you Jane or Jungle Girl, not Zura. There was talk about making a movie of your life. Isn't that amazing?"

"That's too extreme, isn't it?" I questioned.

"Not for Hollywood. Nothing is off the table. Every interesting story is up for grabs. They would eat you up."

"You make them sound like a bunch of hungry lions."

"They are worse than lions. Lions look like tame kittens to the folks in Hollywood and New York. No, Hollywood is much worse," she giggled. "And Zura," she cleared her throat. "I want to thank you for saving my life." She dabbed at her eyes with a part of her sleeve. "Dixon threw me off the ledge for grabbing his arm. I did it so that he would not shoot at you."

Olivia bounced on my back "That's right, Mommy. She saved us too."

I hesitated to answer, considering Alice's actions in the cave, as well as her comforting Olivia to fall asleep at the fire when she was still with Dixon Bain. "I guess we are even," I said.

For the first time, I saw Alice. Not as a threat or a woman too beautiful for me not to be jealous. I saw her as someone who may have some redeeming qualities. It took a lot of courage to put herself in jeopardy for Olivia and me. Now I must return the favor and get her safely out of the jungle.

The snap of a twig and the heavy-footed sounds of men drew my attention. I placed a finger over my lips and grabbed Alice's arm. We ducked into a heavily dense patch of cover.

Dixon Bane and Griffin Stone appeared on the path to the side of us. They must have begun climbing down from the cave just as soon as they threw Alice from the cliff.

The men stalked the area, poking their rifles into the nearby foliage. "They are close," Dixon said. "I'd know Alice's irritating voice anywhere. I swear she was just talking. Never could get her to shut up."

The comments caused an irritation on Alice's face. I shook my head at her to stay still and quiet.

They moved closer and closer, stabbing the vegetation with the end of their rifles.

I motioned for Olivia and Alice to lie flat on the ground in the protection of the dense cover.

We waited without movement.

Within a few minutes, they were above us, shoving their guns into the leaves overhead. A grunt from Dixon revealed his agitation. "Maybe they backed around us," he said peering into our camouflaging cover. "Let's circle back around. They can't be far."

We waited a few minutes before moving from our hiding place. As we were brushing the dirt from our clothes, a familiar whistle echoed in the trees. Several tribesmen gracefully jumped from the trees with barely a sound. I raised a hand for Alice and Olivia to stay and I walked toward the whistle.

"Gamba-Fari," he whispered. Taji appeared from the trees. He raised a finger to his lips to silence me until he reached my location. "Gamba-Fari, you must be careful. You and your family cannot stay here. The bad men are close. Please go before he comes back. Take your daughter, this woman, and go. I will protect you until you reach your home. I have been tracking you for many miles and I will protect you, my sister."

"Taji, do not put yourself in harm for me. Please, you have done enough for me. I can get us home."

"No, you are one of the tribe. We will protect you. You are family. Your child is also my family. These men must not be able to go to your home. They would follow you there and place more of your family at risk. I have seen this warning in a message from the stars. We will kill these evil men before they can hurt anyone else." He disappeared into the trees before I could say another word.

Taji and his men were so well hidden that even I could not spot them in the trees above us.

I turned to walk back to Alice and Olivia and spotted Dixon and Griffin running toward us.

Before I could respond, they were on us. Dixon stepped out of the trees in front of Alice and Olivia's path. It was a mistake to separate from them. "I've got you now, Jane. It's too bad that your daughter has to see you die," Dixon said, pointing a pistol at my head.

His hand swung to Olivia. "Or should I kill the girl first to cause you even more pain? What do you think? Looks like we are back to my original question; who gets to die first? Who should it be, Jane? Maybe it should be Alice for her treachery." His cold eyes glared at a sobbing Alice. She grabbed Olivia's hand and put herself between Olivia and Dixon. "Dix, you will not hurt Olivia!"

Griffin grunted and chuckled. He reached for Alice, grabbing her by the hair to pull her toward himself.

Alice lost her grip on Olivia's hand as she reached for her head. "Stop!" Alice yelled. "Griffin, you're hurting me!"

Before he could respond, something flashed across his face and his eyes widened with surprise. He let go of Alice, who rushed to protect Olivia.

Griffin's mouth hung open with his tongue lying on the side of his lips. It only took a second for him to fall forward, revealing the reason for his quick death. A poisonous dart hung from his left shoulder.

Dixon rushed to Griffin. He reached down to turn him over. Griffin's eyes were set on the sky, devoid of life.

A familiar whistle was sounded between the tribesmen. They came out of their hiding places and surrounded Dixon. Taji jumped from a nearby tree. "You are not welcome in the jungle. You upset our balance. I have spared you for a moment, but my brothers will kill you with one signal from me. Now go and leave my sister and her family alone."

Dixon laughed. "Your sister? She is not your sister; how could she be? It doesn't really matter. She has to die, and you'll not stand in my way!"

I took the opportunity to grab Olivia.

"Jump on my back," I said, bending low for Olivia to climb. "Alice, can you run?" You must keep up with me."

"Don't you worry about me. I want to get as far away from Dix as I can," she said.

But before I could move, a black leopard jumped in my path.

"Don't move!" I hiked Olivia higher on my back. "Nice and easy movements, Alice."

The black leopard jumped onto a downed tree near us. He let out a growl and a hiss. Blood dripped onto my shoulder and I looked up. Hanging awkwardly from the tree was the leopard's kill. A macaque's bloodied torso hung open. Its black-tipped tan coat was covered with its own blood.

I wished I could have shielded Olivia's eyes. "Don't look," I said to her.

I scanned for Taji just in time to see Dixon Bain swing his rifle and hit Taji on the side of the head. Taji stumbled but did not fall.

I saw the dazed look on Taji's face. He looked from me to the panther. "Gamba-Fari, go!" he commanded.

The tribesmen moved closer to Dixon. Their spears were pointed at him and their poisonous darts were ready to find the target. The tribesmen waited too long for the signal from Taji that never came. By the time Taji regained his balance, it was too late.

Dixon had seized the opportunity and swung his gun toward the tribesman and pushed past them. "I'll put a bullet in any of you that tries to follow me!"

He began to retreat without turning his back to the men.

When Dixon was out of sight, he was followed by Taji and his men. Taji was visibly slowed by the blow to his head, but he continued on his quest to protect me. The immediate danger was the hissing leopard. It wasn't the first time I had come face to face with a leopard and its kill. I was so concerned about Dixon and keeping Olivia safe, I forgot to check my environment. It was a stupid mistake.

The leopard's eyes glowed like a full moon against the night sky. Blood dripped from his lips, his teeth bared. A low warning growl filled the air in the sudden silence. All of the animals were on alert.

"Slowly move backward. Do not make a sound. We have to let him know that we have no interest in his kill."

"Mommy, why would we want that meat?" Olivia asked in my ear. "He made a real mess of it."

"Hush now. We are just going to be quiet and move backward slowly."

Olivia did as I asked. Alice could contain her sobs and sniffles.

We didn't get far before the leopard perked up. Something had gotten his attention in the direction that the men traveled.

The leopard hunched low. He lost interest in the three of us when something else caught his attention. The hair on his neck was raised and his low growl hummed louder. He took off in Dixon's direction.

Within seconds, a shot rang out before the sound of the tribesmen's screams followed.

"Taji! I must go back to make sure that Taji is safe. I have to protect my brother! Alice, keep both of you out of sight. Hide! I will be right back." I slid Olivia down to the jungle floor. She grabbed Alice's hand. I wasn't sure who was protecting who. Alice had reached her limit and appeared to be in shock.

I ran as fast as I could into the direction of danger.

I reached the clearing quickly to find Taji on the ground holding his stomach. Blood covered his hands and the front of him.

One of the tribesmen was being dragged backward by the others. His throat was flayed open, his eyes void of life.

Dixon was running in the opposite direction, but he was careless and tripped, landing face-first on the jungle floor. He scrambled for his rifle that was beyond his grasp.

The leopard is an efficient animal. It sprang onto Dixon's back and sank its teeth into the back of Dixon's neck.

The leopard only knows his primal senses. He protects his meal from anything he deems as a threat. There is no rhyme or reason to why the two were the most threatening, but I guessed they made the most movements. Dixon caught his attention, probably by running away.

A gurgling scream escaped from Dixon before the leopard sank his teeth in deeper, stopping the sound mid-scream. The leopard dragged Dixon's limp body in his strong jaws.

This leopard is a man-eater. He snarled a low growl and hissed at me. His topaz eyes shone bright against his dark shiny coat. Beautiful and dangerous, I feared he would tire of Dixon and move on to one of us.

I knelt beside Taji and put pressure on his stomach wound. "Taji, I have to move you quickly before the leopard comes back."

"It is too late. Please, leave me here and my men will tend to me."

"No! I can save you. I just have to get you home. Momma will know what to do. She always knows."

The leopard snarled at us as he dragged the bloodied body of Dixon up a nearby tree.

I covered my mouth and tried not to scream. The leopard planned to eat Dixon. "Taji, I will carry you. We have to move now."

He began to spit blood. "No Gamba-Fari, it is too late. His bloody hands removed his family belt and handed it to me. "Give this to my wife. She needs to know what happened to me."

I handed the belt to one of his men. "We are not far from my home. I will take you there and we will heal you," I said.

I signaled to three of his men to carry him.

Without another word, two Taji's men lifted him by the shoulders and legs.I led the way, followed closely by Taji's men. The other man protected us from behind.

I gave one more backward glance at Dixon's body in the tree and could help but feel sad that, like his father, he allowed anger to destroy himself. I said a silent prayer that Dixon didn't have any other relatives that I would have to worry about coming here to kill me.

Olivia and Alice came out of their hiding place when they saw me. Alice turned white at the sight of Taji.

"Oh, heavens, Zura, who is he?" She looked from me to Taji's tribesmen. "Are we safe with them?" she asked.

"You haven't been safe since you came to Africa. Now let's move.

Take care of Olivia," I called out.

Alice took Olivia's hand and scurried to catch up with me. "But who are they? You never explained when we first saw them." Alice stated.

"This is my brother, Taji. And these men are his tribesman. I have to get him to Momma." I continued to walk quickly.

"What? You are not serious. Your brother? Your mother slept with one of the men from this tribe? How many brothers do you have?" Alice struggled to keep up with me.

"Just two, now let's keep moving." I commanded.

An encroaching storm rumbled above us. The breeze carried the gray clouds in our direction. It started as a few droplets. The cooling soft mist freshened my skin. I looked down to see Taji's blood on my shirt that mixed with the rain. Pink water was running down my arm and soaking my shorts.

We raced back to Momma's favorite field. The elephants were enjoying the rain. They ignored our presence but kept a watchful eye on the lions lying under a tree.

"There's blood in the air. We have to move as fast as we can!"

My footsteps pick up speed and I raced through the shortcut to home.

Olivia screamed when she saw Tim and Isabella's home. "Auntie Izzy! Granny! Help! We need you!"

The tribesmen place Taji on the porch. They remained sentinel at the bottom of the steps.

I wiped my bloodied hands on my shorts and placed my fingers on his neck. I found a weak pulse. He struggled to breathe. Taji's eyes were closed. I hoped he was just unconscious, not passing on to his relatives in the sky.

Seconds passed as the wound continued to diminish him.

"Momma! Izzy! Help, please! I need help!" I screamed. I couldn't control the bleeding, even with all of my strength.

Isabella came running and stopped when she saw Taji lying unconscious on her porch, and me crying over him. I showed Isabella the wound.

"Zura, how are we going to do this? We need your father."

"We have to. He is my brother. I can explain it later. Right now, I need to save his life. I need Momma."

Momma, carrying Charlie, came out of the door. I was never happier to see her.

Charlie reached for me and stopped when he saw the blood covering me and Taji. "Poached man and pink water on Mommy," Charlie said.

"Brother! Olivia ran to Charlie and Momma. "Granny! I was in the jungle with Miss Alice. She let Jeena sleep with me."

"Oh, Olivia. Come to Granny," Momma said and pulled Olivia in for a hug. She kissed her head and looked at me with tears in her eyes.

I removed the extra shirt from my pack and crumbled it into a ball to place under Taji's head. He was still unresponsive to my voice and my touch.

For the first time, Momma looked at Alice. "Why are you here? What's going on? You are supposed to be in the United States. What have you done?" Momma's words sliced the air around us.

Alice swallowed hard under Momma's scrutiny. "It was Dixon's doing. He wanted to get her on the trip to the United States and torture her before he killed her." Alice's cheeks blushed with the stain of guilt. "When Zura refused to leave, he decided to grab Olivia and make her come to him. It was just luck that the men left."

"Luck?" Momma exploded like a panther protecting her young, her attack stance just inches away from Alice's face. "How dare you come to this house!"

Alice dropped her head submissively and her lips trembled. "That's what Dix said."

"Who is Dix?

I faced Momma and saw a hurricane of emotions swirling in her eyes. "Momma, it's Dixon Bain. He is the son of one of the men who kidnapped me and tried to kill me in the jungle, remember?"

Anger, hot as lava showed on Momma's face. It boiled and churned, ready to explode and wipe Alice from this earth.

Isabella cleared her throat and led the children into the house. "Let's go play with your cousins," she said

Momma retreated her assault and stepped closer to Taji and me. "I'm here, Zura. It's going to be alright," Momma confirmed. Without hesitation, she grabs his feet. "Zura, grab under his shoulders," she said with authority. "Izzy! Cover the table with clean linens and open the door, please!"

"I got it, Momma," Isabella called from the house.

Momma took charge. Everything she did was guided by love for her family. "We don't have much time, so everyone does as I say."

Momma waved a hand and the tribesmen immediately understood to take our places and lift Taji to carry him into the house. They placed Taji on top of the kitchen table and walked outside again.

Momma rolled up her sleeves and washed her hands. "Zura, grab my bag on the chair in the living room."

I pushed past Alice, who was standing in the way with her mouth agape. "So much blood," Alice murmured. Her skin turned almost translucent. Alice began to pace, biting on the knuckle of her index finger.

I cannot help but think she is fighting the urge to vomit from the sight of all that blood. I thought quickly before we had another mess on our hands. "Alice, why don't you go help Izzy with the kids," I told her.

"No, I want to be here if you need me."

"We don't need someone who is going to get sick all over the place," Momma stated.

Alice's slight frame stiffened, and she wiped the sweat from her brow. "No, I can do this. There must be some way that I can help him. He saved our lives. I want to help save him."

"Don't get in the way," I answered, rushing to get Momma's bag. When I returned with the bag, I found Momma prepping Taji for surgery. She wiped the blood from his stomach to get a clear picture of the situation.

I held the bag and stared at my mother's skillful hands. They did not shake nor hesitate from the task at hand. Momma locked eyes with me. It is all there on her face. The mask of confidence that I needed her to wear. She was the bridge that held Taji's life to my own.

I felt my own mask begin to crumble under the weight of despair. My paralyzed throat could not speak the words, but Momma knew them anyway. It was there in her eyes. It had always been there, right in front of me. That gentle concern for me and my happiness. The fierceness of a lion's devotion to her cub. She was my wise mother who healed others. In that split second, I could feel my lifetime of scars soften. I could feel the warmth, greater than the sun. It radiated from her.

Momma's authoritative tone helped me have the confidence that she would be able to save Taji's life. She operated on many animals. Humans were not that much different. She continued to dish out orders. "Zura, inside the bag is a long metal scissors with blunt ends, and some other instruments. We will need them sterilized for the surgery. Grab them for me. There is a needle and thread in the inside pocket as well. Make sure you sterilize the instruments and needle thoroughly with alcohol."

"Okay."

"You," Momma turned toward Alice. "Wash your hands and get the alcohol on the top shelf to the left, grab the scalpel from Zura and help her make sure it's sterilized with the rest of the instruments. Everyone be sure we are as clean as possible. We don't want an infection."

Momma poured Tim's imported whiskey over the knife blade and onto Taji's skin before she poured it over her skillful hands. "Zura come here and pour some over your hands. I want you to hold his shoulders still. He can't move. Alice leaned on the lower portion of his thighs, above his knees.."

Momma took a sip from the bottle and swiftly began to make a small incision below the bullet site. She used the scissor-like instrument to open the cut and another instrument to probe for the bullet. Within minutes, she found her mark. "Ah, there you are," she said, pulling the bullet from the wound. She swiftly sewed the wound shut and cleans the rest of Taji's skin with more alcohol. "He has lost a lot of blood."

"Momma that was amazing. I am so glad you were here to do this. I don't know what I would have done." I looked at my mother's proud face. "I have assisted your father with many surgeries over the years. Humans and animals. I am a scientist, you know. Your friend here has a nasty bump on his head as well, but that will heal. We have to let him rest."

Alice disappeared out the door and returned with Taji's tribesmen. They helped me to gently carry Taji to a bedroom on the same floor and lay him down.

I sat by his side, waiting for him to wake. Taji's eyes were closed and he was unresponsive to my touch on his arm. His pulse was weak, but his breathing was steady.

"Fight, Taji. Your family needs you. I need you." I whispered.

My eyes glanced down at the crimson color on my clothes. The scarlet blood trail ran the length of me like the cascading water of the waterfall. So much innocent blood spilled because of hatred and revenge. A cry died in my throat and the numbness took over me. It was my coping mechanism to deal with the past few days.

I couldn't pull myself away from Taji's bedside. I knew that Isabella would see to the care of my children. I had no doubt that Olivia was telling a story of grandeur about her kidnapping and our survival.

My eyes felt incredibly heavy and I began to drift into sleep, lulled by the passing of time and darkening of the room. The silence was like a blanket, covering my wounds that still needed attention. I felt my breath deepen with the calming of my mind. "We are home. We are safe. Bain is gone once more." Momma's words that angered me just a few days earlier were now a comfort to me. "We are home. We are safe," I repeated the words over and over until at last, I slipped into a slumbering fog. Heavy and light at the same time, my mind let go and flew into the heavens, leaving my body wilting in the chair.

It was late in the night before he started to stir. Taji reached out and touched my hand. "Gamba-Fari, there you are," Taji called hoarsely. Taji rested his hand on mine.

"Here I am." I smiled down at him and gently squeezed his hand for reassurance.

"You must rest, sister." Taji's eyes flutter shut. "You will need your strength to handle your deepest fears." Taji was asleep before I could ask him what he meant by *my darkest fears*. I just escaped them. I beat my fear, which happens to be anything or anyone harming my children.

I considered the possibility that his message referred to Matt. My stomach turned into a raging river. Anxiety clenched my chest in a powerful wave stronger than any current. I was sinking in my fear and unable to breathe. I finally gave way to the river and allowed the tears to flow silently down my face.

If the message was to warn me that I was about to lose my beloved husband, I feared that I would crack under the weight and sink down to drown in my own tears.

CHAPTER 8

Momma gently brushed my hair back from my eyes and I stirred.

"Did you sit here all night?" Momma whispered, stroking my cheek.

"I couldn't leave him, Momma. He is my brother."

Momma grinned. "Why is it that whenever you go missing in the jungle, you come back with a brother?" Her lighthearted tone was exactly what I needed. Momma's teasing made me smile and I stretched my stiff body like a cat too long in a tree. "Is everyone else still asleep?" I asked.

"Yes, but I suspect that they will be up soon. Olivia had quite the stories to tell last night. What an imagination that child has. Leopards, gorillas, jumping off the waterfall, swinging across a ravine, you name it, she thought it up." Momma said searching my eyes.

"Sadly, they are all true." I stood and took my mother's hand.

Momma's face paled. "That's what I was afraid of, Zura." She cleared her throat. "Promise that you will be a better mother and listener to her than I was for you."

"Momma, if I have learned anything in the last few days, it is how unfair I have been to you. I now understand your pain and your inability to cope with my stories of torture. It's so hard to hear those things when they happen to your child. It's like a part of you has been broken right along with them."

"That is exactly why I struggled to talk about the hurt that you endured."

"I know that now. Never doubt what an amazing mother you are," I said.

"Speaking of hurt, let me take a look at your leg. Olivia said that you used ants to stitch up a wound." Momma shook her head. "Just like your father."

"Where do you think I got the idea to do it?" I moved my leg forward so that Momma could examine my handy work with the ants. With their heads still intact, I was pretty proud of my ingenuity. Momma's scowl sang a different tune. "Your friend here is sleeping peacefully. Let's go clean up your wounds and get those ants out of the way so that I can stitch it properly," she said.

Momma led me to the kitchen table. "Take a seat."

I pulled out a chair and sat with my legs crossed. I had a feeling that I may be sitting endlessly as Momma looked me over from head to toe.

She lifted the back of my top to look for the cause of my blood-soaked shirt. "Where is it? Where are you hurt?" Momma frantically looked for an injury.

I grabbed her arm. "That's not my blood," I said. "It's Taji's."

She made little grunting noises that revealed her concern. She scrubbed and cleaned my abrasions and the dried blood from Taji's injury. "I can't tell what's your blood and what's his. It's all mixed together."

"You have no idea," I said, remembering the ceremony where we commingled our blood.

"What's that?" Momma questioned.

"Well, remember when I told you that Taji was my brother?"

"Yes." Momma stopped and braced herself for my answer.

"Taji's chief wanted me to marry his son in order to pass through their land. It would also give me the protection of the tribe."

"But you are married. How could you marry someone else? Oh, you didn't!" Momma looked shaken.

"Momma, give me some credit. I would never marry someone else. I love Matt. Taji came up with a way to help me by making me his sister. There was a ceremony."

"What kind of ceremony?" Momma asked.

I hesitated to tell my mother about the co-mingling of our blood, but I had no other choice. "The ceremony combined our families into one."

"And just how did you combine our families?" Momma questioned, igniting her motherly flame.

"Well, by blood." I shrugged as if it was no big deal.

"Blood? You combined blood with a stranger?"

"Momma, he can't be a stranger and my brother at the same time. That's just silly," I diverted my answer.

"Oh, how could you?"

"I did it for Olivia. I would have done anything to save my little girl."

Momma paused and let out a deep breath. "Of course, you would. You would have walked through fire to save her."

"I did everything but walk through fire. Olivia's stories are the truth. We were almost killed by a gorilla, she grabbed a vine and swung across a ravine at the same time that I was trying to figure out how to get us both across. She just did it. I think instinctually."

"And the waterfall? Did you really jump off that waterfall?"

"It was either that or be shot by Dixon Bain. Besides, Olivia told me to do it. She actually said, 'do it, Mommy.' She has always known about my jungle adventures and she had way more confidence in my abilities than I will ever have in myself." I laughed. "She told me that I was Jane and to jump because she is a really good swimmer."

The blood drained from her face, causing Momma to become ghostly pale. "How can you laugh at that?"

"What else am I going to do? She was right. She swims like a fish. Momma, she soared unafraid and even asked if we could do it again sometime. I fear I have been a bad influence on my child. But we lost her monkey, Jeena, in the fall. I think she died when I jumped."

"Does Olivia know?"

"I didn't have the heart to tell her."

Momma grew silent. She continued addressing my numerous injuries.

During the ordeal, I never stopped to feel the pain. Now, I could trace them all over my legs, arms and shoulder. Some wounds are barely noticeable, but others caused a searing pain when she cleaned them. I winced without compassion from Momma. She instinctively continued the process until she was sure that no infection would ensue.

My hands impulsively clenched, and I bit my lip. "It burns!"

"Zura, I can't risk you getting bacteria in these wounds. They could become infected. Sit still and let me do this," Momma warned. "You have purple bruises on your shoulder, legs, everywhere. And these cuts! They are deep. What's this?" Momma touched a very sore lump on the side of my forehead. I flinched and tried to pull away. She was relentless in her assault of my lacerations. More burning, more scrubbing and more pain until I could no longer take it. I tried to stand, but she pushed me back into the seat. "We are not done," she said. The ants will be the worst part. The rest is done."

Isabella joined us in the kitchen and sat across from me.

I wrinkled up my face from the pain. "Oh good, I have a witness to the torture going on in this kitchen. Tell me, Izzy, is there any speck of skin left on me, or has she scrubbed it clean off of my bones?"

"I think there is a spot left that you might be sitting on," she teased.

"Trust me, when she's done, that will be gone too," I turned to face Momma's stern gaze.

Isabella giggled at Momma and me and stood to start some hot water for tea. "Zura, you need to replenish your fluids from your trip. Drink this."

Isabella handed me a glass of the cloudy-white liquid. She knew it's one of my favorite juices.

"Soursop fruit, this will help me endure this harsh punishment."

I drank the juice as if I hadn't tasted fluids in weeks. My parched mouth eagerly swallowed every drop. Satisfied, I wiped my mouth with the back of my hand. "That was so good. Thank you, Izzy," I smiled.

I felt the pinch of the needle, followed by the tugging of the thread that Momma carefully pulled to close the gaping gash in my leg. Again and again, she repeated the process with precision.

"There you are," Momma boasted. "Good as new."

We gathered around the kitchen table and waited for the children to wake. I brought some tea to the tribesmen who had vigilantly stood outside through the night and told coaxed them inside to see Taji so they would know he was alright.

The tranquil silence shattered when we heard the thumping of Olivia running down the hall and bouncing down the stairs in her bare feet. She ran into my arms.

"Morning, Mommy!"

"Good morning, Olivia." I wrapped her in my arms and kissed her head.

"Can we go to look for Jeena this morning? You said that we could find her after we got home."

I looked from Momma then back to Olivia's innocent face. She stood on her tiptoes and twirled in her night dress. There is something intoxicating about her energy. She's so full of life and able to put yesterday's sorrows easily from her mind. It's like it never happened. There didn't seem to be an ounce of fear or anxiety from our adventure. I will be sure to watch for signs that she needs to talk. I'll be there to help her cope with the tragedy she has seen.

"You want to go back into the jungle so soon? We just got home. Let's give it a couple of days, alright?"

"We can't Mommy! Jeena doesn't have a couple of days. She needs me now."

"Let's just wait. Jeena will be able to take care of herself. She is a wild animal, Olivia. She has the instincts to survive."

"So do you. That's why I need you to help me find her." Olivia became agitated by my hesitation. "Would you have waited a couple of days to find me?"

"Of course not. I came right away."

"Why?"

"Why did I come right away?" I asked.

Olivia nodded her head.

"Because you are my child and I love you."

"And Jeena is my baby monkey and I love her." Olivia crossed her arms to make her point.

Momma burst out laughing. "She painted you right into a corner. She's just like you, Zura."

I could not help but smile down at my little girl. "Let's do this. Why don't we look for her near the house for two more days and if she doesn't come back, we will go out to find her, okay?"

Olivia placed her pointer finger on her lips and looked up toward the ceiling. "What about one more day?" she asked.

I am grateful for the extra time. "Agreed," I said, taking her hand in mine and giving it a little kiss. I want to check on Taji. Momma, can you feed the tribesmen? They must be hungry."

"Sure. I invited them in last night, but they preferred to sleep outside. I am not sure what they will eat, and they do not speak our language."

"They will be grateful for anything that you provide. Especially some of the smoked meats."

I grabbed some soursop juice and went to the bedroom that Taji was using to recuperate. I leaned on the door frame and watched him. He was awake and looking out the window at the rising sun. He appeared to feel better than he did last night. The bandages on his stomach were not showing signs of recent bleeding. For that, I was grateful.

Taji turned his head and saw me staring at him. "Are you troubled, Gamba-Fari?" He spoke hoarsely.

"No, I'm not troubled. You look so much better this morning. I brought you some juice," I said walking over to him and helping him to take a few sips.

It is very good. Soursop is my favorite," he said.

"It's mine too."

I placed a hand on his forehead to check for a fever, which could mean an infection. His skin glistened with sweat that I suspected was coming more from pain than infection.

"Are you feeling alright?" I asked.

"I am fine. Just sore in my stomach. I will heal and be perfectly fine. Do not worry about me."

"You saved our lives, Taji. I will always be grateful for you," I said laying my hand on his arm. "Imagine the stories that we will tell our children. Your tribe will be proud of your selflessness."

"Yes, well, Imani will be happy when I return."

"Taji, last night you told me that I had to gain strength for what is to come. What did you mean?"

"I will tell you a secret that may be hard to understand. I was visited by an ancestor from the sky before you came to our village. I was given a message about you."

"About me?"

"Yes," Taji struggled to sit up. I propped pillows behind him to help him with his efforts.

"Ah, thank you. That is much better," he said. "The message spoke about a strong warrior that will need my help. I was to make sure to protect the warrior with my life. It also said that hardship and mourning will come upon the warrior."

"Mourning? How can this message be about me? I am not mourning the loss of the men from the jungle, and Olivia is very much alive. I am certainly not mourning the men from my childhood either. You know about my struggles, the lifetime of sorrow over Tembo. Could it be about him? The only…" The words caught in my throat. Matt, Tim, and Father could be the reason for the message. Maybe if I didn't speak the words, they would never come to life. I needed the words to die in my throat and vanish from my thoughts.

Taji looked worriedly at me. He saw my raw emotions trying to expose themselves and me pushing them back down. He took my hand and traced the newly formed scar on my palm. The one that united us by blood. "We are here together for a reason, Gamba-Fari. You must believe that the ancestors in the stars have not left you to be alone. They watch over you."

"I cannot lose any of them. I need all of them," I said desperately.

Taji looked away. He was stalling and that scared me even more.

"What are you not telling me, Taji?"

"I do not have the answers that you seek."

"Well, how can I get the answers?"

"You wait for fate to reveal itself. That's what all of us must do. I am sorry, Gamba-Fari, I cannot help with this."

"I know you can't"

"I must go home now. I am healed enough for the travel."

"I will take you."

"You must stay here. Your family needs you. My brothers will take me."

We stared at each other for a moment. An unspoken message between the silence confirmed my fears.

Momma stepped into the room with her hands holding a tray of food. "I brought you something to eat, Taji. You need your strength."

"Thank you for your care." Taji smiled up at my mother. "And for saving my life."

"For what you did for my daughter, I should be thanking you. You will always be welcome here at Wild Hearts. You and your family. And I hope that you will bring them to visit us one day."

Taji nodded and began to sip the broth that Momma provided.

Isabella entered the room holding a basket of clean linens. She placed the basket on the floor next to a chair and began to put the linens away. "Taji, more of your men have just arrived. They will not come into the house. They are at the tree line with a few more men."

"Yes, they've come to bring me home."

I looked confusedly at Taji. "But how did they know?"

"Gamba-Fari, not everything can be explained with words. Sometimes the vibrations of the earth and the connections of people just know. Now help me to my feet and I will go with my people."

I put my hands under his arm and helped to get him to his feet. He moved slowly, but on his own. When we stepped onto the porch, I saw the men waiting at the tree line. They carried their spears and looked patiently in our direction. I raised my hand in greeting and they copied my gesture.

Taji turned toward me and placed his hands on both of my arms. He smiled as he gently squeezed my arms. "I leave you now, Gamba-Fari. This will not be the end for us. I will see you in the stars."

"We can visit. You can come back anytime you want. I could..."

"No, this will be the end for this lifetime. But I will see you in the next. Our lives are different, and you must follow this path. Your path. You will be tested. Your faith, your patience and your love. Do not despair. It will be as it is meant to be."

Taji turned and walked away without another word. I found my feelings torn. I wanted to run after him to make him tell me what his message meant. I also didn't really want to find out the answer.

Momma placed an arm around my shoulder. "What was he talking about, Zura?"

"It is nothing Momma," I answered, staring at Taji when he gave me one last look and disappeared into the trees.

I heard Olivia come out of the screened door with a slam. There she stood proudly holding Jeena in her arms. "Look Mommy, Jeena came home just like you said!" she said, stroking Jeena's disheveled fur.

I had no idea how the monkey found her way back to us. The only thing that I can think of is she has this connection with Olivia.

"How?" Momma whispered in my ear.

"Maybe the monkey sees Olivia as its mother or caretaker. I've never seen anything like it."

"I have."

"You have? When?"

Momma let out a hearty laugh. "With you. You cannot discount the actions of Tembo and Cha-cha when you were a child. They would have given their lives to save yours."

The memory of my beloved animal friends was bittersweet. "Yes," I answered, looking at the ground. "I suppose you are right. I think it is time for the children and me to make our way home. Running back and forth between here and home doesn't make sense now that Taji was healed."

"What about that Alice woman? Is she going with you too?"

I looked over at Alice. Her hair flew freely about her face and her smile was genuine. She sat on the porch holding Kora and Kara on her lap. Charlie was showing her a bug that he captured in his tiny hands. She didn't pull away like she would have done just a few short days earlier. Alice looked in my direction and with a wave and a smile, she melted my apprehensions. Maybe in another world we could have been great friends, maybe even sister-like. But I knew she would be leaving soon and there was no reason to get any more attached than my children and I have become.

I waved back and she stood, putting the twins on the step beside Charlie and kissing both of them on the head.

Alice walked the short distance to join Momma and me. "Good morning!" she called.

Momma let out a disdainful grunt and crossed her arms.

"Be nice," I whispered for only Momma to hear.

"It won't be soon enough for her to go back to the United States."

"Momma, please," I sighed.

Alice reached us looking nervously from Momma to me and back again. She was wringing her hands like she didn't know what to do with them. A blush slowly crept up Alice's neck and cheeks. "I, uh, want to say that I am sorry for my part in what happened to Olivia and you, Zura."

"Alice, we have already discussed this. I forgave you, remember?"

Her eyes darted to Momma as the words blurted out like a strike from a snake. "I want to stay. Here with all of you."

The silence between us stilled the breeze. No movement from anyone, we just stared at one another.

Momma stepped forward. "You do not belong here," she stated without compassion.

"I could belong here," Alice did not falter.

"No, you cannot. We do not need your kind here," Momma said unrelentingly.

I touched Momma's arm and slid my body between them. "Momma, please, let me speak." I turned toward Alice. "Alice, it's true. This is no place for someone that doesn't know what they are doing."

Alice hung her head in defeat. I saw something there, in her eyes. There was a hurt that went beyond Momma and me. There was abandonment and a lifetime of loneliness that showed in the tear that trickled down her cheek.

I placed my hand on Alice's shoulder. "Surely you have family waiting for you at home, Alice. You do, don't you?"

With a head shake, Alice looked into my eyes. The dark and moody storm behind her gaze gave way to a torrent of tears. "I have no one. I do not belong anywhere. But I like it here. I love the children. They bring me so much joy. And I want to watch them grow. Please, let me stay."

I looked at Momma and she rolled her eyes at me. "Why do I get the feeling that you are bringing an injured animal home with you again?"

I smiled at Momma's perspective. I do have a soft spot for the weak and injured. Right then and there, there was nothing as weak and injured as Alice. "You can come home with me, Alice. I could use the help with Matt gone. You can muck the stalls and help me tend to the animals."

Alice grabbed my arms. "I'll do anything! Thank you, Zura. Thank you!"

"Can you help me get the children ready to go?" It's time we returned home for good."

Alice practically floated as she walked toward the children. I saw her whisper in Olivia's ear. Olivia hugged her and ran into the house. She picked up Charlie and followed Olivia into the house.

"I hope you know what you are doing," Momma stated.

I kissed her cheek and walked toward the house to gather our things.

CHAPTER 9

Time was passing quickly at home with my children and Alice. I tended to the stalls in the barn and heard the squealing and laughing coming from outside.

I opened the barn door enough to let little Maji wander out to join the fun. The squealing and yelling continued. I opened the barn door the rest of the way to see why Olivia continued to scream with delight.

Everyone was looking toward the hill and I turned to see what all the excitement was about. My heart pounded out of my chest with the sight of him. His handsome face stole my breath. I watched Matt walk toward us with his natural swagger. I smiled at the way his suspenders hung at his sides with his crisp white shirt unbuttoned just three buttons from the top.

Matt saw me and his steps quickened. The closer we got to each other the more I saw the despair on his face. There is no sunshine in the darkness of his mood. He stopped and breathed in deep, unable to continue his steps.

This is not the reunion that I had planned in my mind. My husband had been gone for too long. I should be wrapped in his arms, not watching him crumble before my eyes.

No amount of hesitation could eliminate the inevitable. I continued until I was standing directly in front of him.

He dropped his suitcase and opened his arms. I fell into them without hesitation.

Matt ran his hands into my hair loosening my ponytail. He breathed in deep. "Oh, how I have missed you, Zura," he said. I ran as fast as I could from Tim's house,"

"I've missed you too. But I am glad that you are back. There is so much that I have to tell you."

I pulled from our embrace to look into his eyes. They are tired and worried.

Matt opened his mouth to speak, then shut it just as quickly.

"What is it? What's wrong? I asked.

"Zura, I don't know how to tell you something."

"Tell me quickly not slowly. I cannot stand to hear what troubles you in pieces. Just say it."

"It's your father, Zura. He is very sick."

"What's wrong?" I stepped away from Matt and searched his eyes once more for the answer.

"It's his heart."

"I will go to him and stay with Father and Momma until he gets better."

"You can't do that."

"Why can't I do that?"

"Because your father is not here."

"Well, where is he?"

"Peter is in a hospital in New York."

"New York! You left my father with Tim in New York? Matt you are not making sense. Why would you leave him there?"

"Because he is too ill to travel. Tim is home as well. Peter has had surgery for his heart. They are trying to save him. He took a turn for the worse and began calling for you and Momma. He needs you, Zura. You must go to him."

I staggered back from the crashing wave of despair stealing my air, my fear drowning out the sounds around me.

"Zura, listen." Matt touched my arm. "You must get ready. You have to pack. Tim is going to your mother's home to help her get ready. Then the truck will come here to pick you up. That's why I ran to you. I couldn't wait for the driver to wait for your mother before coming here to get you. There is a private plane waiting for you. Tim has taken care of getting you into the country. Let's go get you ready."

"Tim left too? How could you both just leave him like that?"

Because Tim needs to be at home for Isabella and the baby. I have to be here for our children. Tim has arranged constant care nurses for him until you get there. We don't have a lot of time to get you to the plane."

Matt took my hand, grabbed the suitcase, and led me quickly down the hill to a waiting Olivia and Charlie. He scooped up Charlie, and Olivia latched to his leg. "Daddy!" Olivia yelled.

Matt stared at Alice in disbelief. "I thought you were going back to New York with us. Why were you and Alex's men not with us?"

Alice hung her head in shame. Her nervous hands sweep through her wild, disorderly hair. Before Alice could respond, Olivia excitedly began to jump in place. "I know, I know! She was with me, Daddy. Oh, and that bad man in the jungle. But Mommy came and rescued me. Then the mean gorilla tried to eat us, but the bad man shot him. We ran away and I jumped real far over the hole in the ground. Mommy took me to the waterfall and guess what, Daddy!"

Matt's wide-eyes stare at me in disbelief. "What, Olivia?"

'We jumped! Right off the waterfall so the bad man couldn't shoot us. Alice saved us from him shooting, but we jumped right off and when we were in the water, Mommy said I swam like a fish. I lost my baby Jeena, but she came home. It's not too far from the waterfall to home, so Jeena found me again. Then Mommy's friend, Taji, got shot and his men carried him until we got to Auntie Izzy's house." Olivia giggled.

"Charlie thought Mommy was poached! Cuz of all the blood and the pink water. That was funny, right Mommy?"

Charlie lay a hand on Matt's face. "Mommy got poached. She had pink water," he chuckled.

I nodded at Olivia but watched Matt's face as his shocked expression deepened and turned to horror.

"There you have it," I said. "That's what we did while you were gone." I turned without further explanation for Matt. There was no time to explain the events of the past few weeks.

Matt cleared his voice. "Taji?"

I turned toward Matt. "Taji is from the Swavendi Tribe. You probably should know I am now a tribe woman. I had to become part of them."

"How did you join a tribe?"

I sighed. "I don't have time to explain. I must pack. There are only two ways. Marry the chief's son or become a sister of a tribesmen." I turned and walked toward the porch.

I heard Matt calling after my departure. "Which one did you do?"

I hurry up the porch steps, taking two at a time and throwing open the screened door. I ran up the stairs to the bedroom. Matt joined me in our bedroom and laid his suitcase on the bed. He emptied his clothing. "Here you go. Place your things in here."

I began to search through my sparse clothing. Tan or gray shorts, button-down shirts, and shabby boots littered the floor. "Matt, I need Alice. Can you get her please?"

Matt ran down the stairs and left the house with a bang of the screened door. I hear the door open with its familiar creak. "I am coming, Zura," Alice said making her way up the stairs.

I felt broken and ready to shatter into a million pieces. "Help me," I pleaded.

Alice quickly assessed the disheveled situation on the floor and miraculously found a few items and folded them before placing them in the suitcase. "Don't worry. I have a few pairs of pants that are too long for me. They were Isabella's and she gave them to me to wear. They will fit."

"That's good, I can just wear these shirts. It will be fine."

Alice stopped to face me. "Zura, it's winter time there. It's going to be cold."

"Cold?"

"Yes, probably even snowy. We will use Matt's suit jackets to keep you warm until we can get you a coat when we land."

"I have never owned a coat in my life. "Matt's clothing will be fine. I don't really care about the clothing. I just have to get to my father."

"I understand. That's why I have decided to go with you. I am not much help here. But in the United States, I can help you navigate the city and streets. Not to mention the people."

"You would do that for me?"

"Zura, I owe you my life. Yes, I will do this for you. Think of it as a penance for some of my sins. It's the least I can do."

She disappeared to Olivia's room and I heard her opening drawers. Within minutes, she was back with her suitcase. "I have things for you in this one as well. Are we ready?"

I nodded and looked at Alice for a moment. "Thank you," I said.

Alice put out her hand to shake mine and I pulled her into a sisterly hug.

When I pulled away, I saw the biggest smile and a solitary tear slide down her cheek. "No thanks needed."

Matt stood in the doorway watching us. "Very odd," he stated. "I thought you hated each other."

"We did," Alice and I said in unison.

The sound of the truck's horn hurried our pace.

The children were in the kitchen eating a snack. Saying goodbye to them was like pouring salt in the wound. I hugged and kissed them both. I will miss them dearly. Nothing could prepare me for saying goodbye to my children without knowing when I would see them again.

Matt walked me to the truck without a word. We silently embraced, the battle with our emotions raging. Matt and I lost the fight quickly. Our reunion would have to wait.

Matt sighed. "I will miss you."

"I'll miss you too."

Olivia ran toward the truck and was swinging the rag doll from the cave. "Here, Mommy." She held the dolls out for me to take. "You can have your baby doll for your trip. You might need her to sleep with you, so you don't get scared of the dark."

"Thank you, Olivia. I will bring her back with me soon."

"And maybe if you want, you can bring me a new baby," Olivia smiled.

There was nothing else to say and I stepped up into the truck to sit next to Alice. I could not prolong a goodbye that was breaking my heart.

We drove to Momma's home and found her and Tim waiting on her porch. Momma nervously twisted her handkerchief in her shaking hands. She was so distraught that she didn't seem to notice that Alice was with us. Maybe she just didn't care.

Tim handed me an envelope. "You will need these. They are papers for you to enter the country and money for your trip. Don't ask about the papers, I arranged it out of necessity. I have arranged for a car to pick you up at the private airport. The driver is Calvin Lewis. He handles my financial transactions in the States. He will make sure that you have a place to stay close to the hospital and will take care of anything you need."

I nodded and handed the envelope to Alice.

Tim made eye contact with Alice and questions swarmed in his eyes. "Why are you here? I thought you were coming with us to the States."

I let out a sigh. "Tim, I don't have time to explain, but I will when we get home, alright?"

"Sure, you go now. Love you, Momma. Love you, Zura." Tim pounded on the truck and we began to move. The truck ride jostled us back and forth for the hour drive to the airport. There is a man standing outside of the plane when we pull up. He opened the truck door for us and bowed. "Ladies, I assure you, you are in good hands. I will get you safely to your destination."

The truck driver unloaded our luggage and carried it to be loaded onto the plane.

Momma and Alice quickly boarded the plane. I hesitated at the bottom step.

"Zura," Momma called. "We have to go. Come on now. I know you are scared. We will face whatever has happened together. Now come here and we can go."

I have never left my home in Africa, never thought about leaving Wild Hearts.

I looked down at the side of the plane. It looked like a cave to me, but with no way out. Like a prison or a coffin. The thought of flying never crossed my mind and I found myself paralyzed in my tracks. My heart beat wildly in my chest. The fear was unexpected but real. As real as the sudden shaking of my hands and the burning heat that caused me to sweat. It's as real as the fluid that trickled down my back. There was no logic to my feelings, no reason for the paralysis.

Momma appeared at the doorway and extended her hand. "Come, it will be alright."

I took her hand and let out a cleansing breath. Without thinking further, I stepped onto the plane and took a seat between Momma and Alice.

When the plane took off, Momma held my hand.

We were in the air soaring like a bird into the sky, into the clouds that hung in the air around us.

We began the long flight to the United States.